The Tippling Tales

Mike Bellis

This is a work of fiction. Names characters, businesses, events, places and incidents are either the products of the author's imagination or used in a fictional manner. Any resemblance to actual persons living or dead or actual events is purely coincidental.

This book is for Hayley and Jessie
My beautiful girls

A massive thank you to Desh Kapur
for believing in me all those years ago in the tiny
cottage in Dolgarrog. Happy days.

A very special thank you to Diana Golding for all her
hard work, support, and kind words about my book.

Thanks to Charlie Finch for encouraging me and
helping me to complete my book.

Also, a massive thank you to everyone who listened
to me rambling on about my stories over the years
and encouraged me to complete
The Tippling Tales.

Thank you all so much.

Sometimes dreams come and go but this nightmare would stay in the boy's head forever. A dream of goblin-like creatures, spells, wizardry and of course the evil Master Huckle. I hope your nightmares are kind to you tonight and you sleep well.

Welcome to
The Tippling Tales

Chapter 1
The Nightmare

The grey coloured pebble-dashed house on Old
Black Street Estate looked gloomy in the mid-
December early morning rain. A violent storm was
brewing in the mountains above and was heading
down the valley towards the small village of Bont.

The local town about ten miles away had suffered
a severe battering the night before, the biggest storm
for over a hundred years people said, and it was now
about to thrash into the small village. Three houses
from the town had had their roofs torn off and the
local river had burst its banks, causing floods the
town had never experienced before.

The wind raced down the small valley like a pack
of rabid wolves and howled through the dark
alleyways in Old Black Street Estate.

Work clothes left out on the washing line from
the calm day earlier danced together like ghosts in the
night's black sky. The storm was approaching with a
vengeance, it clapped and thundered in the lightning
light show. The orange glow of the street light next to
number 38 flickered on and off in the wind, revealing
a pile of old cardboard boxes and rubbish dumped up

against the broken cast iron garden gate.

The thunder shook the house as the boy awoke in a cold sweat in his dark bedroom. The storm outside roared into his ears like a lion and rattled the metal bedroom window frames in anger.

Daniel opened his blurry blue eyes and sat up in his tiny box bedroom. He gazed solemnly into the dark struggling to come to terms with the horrible nightmare that had awoken him so abruptly. Shadows from the trees outside danced around the room as his imagination started to run wild.

Daniel sat up in his bed clutching his blankets in his hands, pulling them up to his face. The boy was petrified as his nightmare along with the storm exploded like fireworks deep in his mind. He vaguely remembered strange black goblin-like creatures. Some had sharp gnashing teeth, others with evil piercing black eyes. In his misty dream, he saw the tall dark figure of a man wearing a large black cloak holding a staff like a shepherd, but this man was no shepherd. The tall figure was surrounded by thirteen horsemen guarding him as if their lives depended on it. The horses snorted loudly as steam rose from their sweaty backs.

Daniel trembled and tried to blank the nightmare from his mind. He closed his eyes tightly, but his nightmare was still there, this would not go away easily. Shivering with total fear he slowly slid down his bed and watched the shadows dance around his tiny cold bedroom. The storm outside was gathering pace and was now getting closer and louder by the minute.

The street lights outside flickered off for a minute as Daniel's bedroom turned into complete darkness.

The thunder clouds bounced together and roared in the skies above his room. A flash of lightning entered the small box room as Daniel held his blankets close towards his tired, bloodshot eyes. Another flash of lightning lit up the room for a second like a fireball. The boy's mind started to play some wicked tricks, or were they tricks?

In the corner of the room, only five foot away, stood the dark grey figure of the man he had seen in his nightmare only five minutes earlier.

The boy, stiff with fear looked on with bulging eyes. The figure stood motionless as lightning lit up his features. The man grimaced and gazed at the boy.

Daniel's eyes opened widely as he slowly pulled the blankets above his head and slid into a ball in the middle of his bed. He shivered with fear as thunder clapped again above the house louder than he had ever heard before.

The storm was here and tried desperately to enter the room to visit the boy's nightmare. Daniel lay sealed in his cocoon and didn't move an inch. The bed was soaked with sweat as the boy waited, for what seemed like an eternity. At least an hour of endless time had passed before Daniel slowly decided to pull the blankets away from his face. The storm outside cheered loudly with claps of thunder as he emerged from his wet sweat sodden bed. The dark figure had gone just as quickly as it had appeared. The mind is a cruel tool of torture.

Daniel laid back in his bed and listened to the madness outside. His eyelids started to get heavier and heavier, but no way was he going back into that nightmare. Daniel fought hard, but as we all know sleep fights harder. His heavy eyelids flickered opened and closed as the orange street lights outside turned off bringing total darkness.

The boy was now asleep again, the heaviest sleep of his life. His nightmare and his vision were somehow erased from his mind for now. Daniel slept quietly as the storm raged outside.

Strange and weird things were about to happen in the small village of Bont. History was about to be changed and people would talk about this story for centuries. Daniel Hawthorn's nightmare wasn't erased, Daniel Hawthorn's nightmare was just about to begin.

Chapter 2
The Hawthorns

Daniel Hawthorn was 11 years old and had always been skinny and frail. His arms and legs were as thin as matchsticks. His hair was straight black like his mother's and his complexion was winter grey.

Early morning dim light shone in through the slightly mouldy ripped net curtains in Daniel's bedroom. Wind and rain crashed violently against the small windowpanes at number 38 Old Black Street.

It was Monday the 19th of December and the weather was atrocious.

Daniel lay in his bed and listened to the elements outside. The storm from the town up the valley was still battering the small village with a vengeance.

Daniel yawned then shivered as he pulled his blankets up towards his chin and lay motionless listening to the chaos outside. The clock ticked away on his bedside cabinet like a leaking tap waiting for the vocal storm inside the house to begin. 8.22am soon turned to 8.32am and still all the Hawthorn family weren't up. Daniel would be late for school yet again.

The metal garden gate outside slammed loudly against the garden wall as a gust of wind tried to rip it off its hinges. The latch on the gate like everything else in and around the old council house was broken.

Across the road from number 38, Mrs Davies opened her front door and quickly snatched the bottle of milk from the doorstep closing the door quietly behind her. Mrs Davies was a good mother and wife. Two girls Jenny and Jane, and a husband who didn't drink, the Davies's were lucky. No such luxury in number 38.

The slamming of the garden gate awoke Mrs Hawthorn from her comatose drunken sleep. She sat up in her bed and coughed, a rattle that rose from her deep dark tarred lung jungle. She shook Mr Hawthorn and in her grainy voice, told him to get up. Mr Hawthorn snarled then turned over and shuffled his dull yellow cigarette stained pillow. Red veins like roads on a road map covered his ageing complexion. A man of only 51 years old but this morning looked more like 91. The late night's heavy drinking and unhealthy living had definitely done its job on Mr Hawthorn. Saliva dripped from his chapped lips and slid onto his pillow like a large garden slug. With foul-smelling breath, he coughed his first phlegm of the day. The bedroom stunk of smoke and stale beer. Mrs Hawthorn coughed again as she lazily gazed over at the clock on the bedside cabinet. She squinted her eyes then bellowed the first of the many screams of the day

"Harold we're late again" screamed the agitated wife, tossing the blankets from the old spring bed onto the bedroom floor.

She quickly scrambled into her factory clothes that had been left on the bedroom floor since the end of her shift on Friday afternoon. Her weekend spent in the Highwayman's Arms was now just a blur in her muddled mind. Her clothes smelt stale and mouldy. The mouldy stench of Mrs Hawthorn was the talk of the factory where she worked. She wasn't well-liked, her sickly mouldy stench of stale clothes was enough to make a dog grimace.

"Harold you up yet?" bellowed Helen once again as she washed her face in the freezing cold water in the bathroom.

Lightning lit up the bathroom like a floodlight as Helen gazed at her ageing appearance in the dust-covered mirror.

Harold snarled then slowly sat up in his bed and lit his first rolled up cigarette of the day. The smoke rose to the top of the bedroom ceiling trying itself to escape the stench of the foul-smelling room. Harold puffed on his death stick then retched and dropped it into a mug by the side of his bed. The stick hissed its last gasp of life as it joined the graveyard of about seventy cigarettes in the week- old cold tea.

Helen opened her bloodshot eyes with her fingers and gazed at the figure in the mirror in front of her. A tear dripped from the tear duct of the once beautiful long dark-haired lady and crashed onto the bathroom floor like a brick. The beer wine and whisky were slowly but surely sucking the life out of them.

Harold walked slowly from the foul-smelling bedroom and into the bathroom. Helen shook herself as she passed her husband on the landing and rushed downstairs to fill the kettle.

Thunder shook the house like an earthquake as

the rain bashed against the kitchen window. Daniel sat in his bed trying desperately to remember his weird dream, he remembered waking up and listening to the storm but as for the dream, his mind was blank. Suddenly from the kitchen, the shouting began

"Daniel are you up yet? Its 8.45."

Daniel sat on his bed and gazed out of his window at the dark Monday morning rain. The wind and rain tried their hardest to enter the small bedroom at number 38. Droplets of rain pushed their way through a small crack in the window onto the windowsill forming a small pool of water, the pool rippled and looked like a new world had been created, maybe it had?

The curtains moved eerily like a ghostly figure as the wind pushed its way through the draughty bedroom.

Daniel put on his bedside lamp and looked around for his school clothes.

Suddenly from nowhere like an invisible wisp of smoke the stench of the bedroom next door raced into his nostrils. Daniel gagged and quickly put his hand over his mouth and nose. His mouth filled with saliva and he swallowed hard.

Mr Hawthorn slowly emerged from the bathroom and rocked from side to side as he walked along the landing and back towards his bedroom. As he approached the boy's door, he banged on it loudly and raised his voice

"Get up boy," the drunk screamed, coughing his guts up in the process and retching as last night's beer and cigarettes raced towards his palette.

Daniel removed the blankets and an old coat off his bed and then started to get changed into his foul-smelling, unwashed school uniform. He could hear his father coughing and spitting into his handkerchief in the next room. Then the verbal storm began, as it did every morning after a night in the Highwayman's Arms. Helen would always start it, saying Harold was spending too much time and money in the gloomy dark back room of the Highwayman's Arms. What he did there she didn't know, but what she did know she didn't like.

"Do you realise what time it is Harold?" Helen bellowed towards her once-beloved husband.

She quickly slapped on some makeup trying desperately to hide her ageing appearance. Her eyes were still bloodshot, and her face had turned red with anger.

Harold rolled downstairs totally ignoring his bellowing wife and poured himself a mug of tea. He bit into a piece of last night's supper, which was on the draining board. Cold runny egg on toast. He belched again as he gulped down the rest of his large mug of tea. It was now 8.50am and both Mr and Mrs Hawthorn were at least an hour late for work.

The Hawthorns both worked in the metal factory in the next village called Garrog that employed about three hundred local people.

Harold fumbled around in the hallway looking for his works jacket mumbling to himself about his nagging wife. Egg deposits hung onto his chin as he placed the grimy, oil-stained jacket over his slightly hunched back. Helen pushed passed him and impatiently tried to open the jammed front door. Harold shrugged her aside and the arguing continued louder than ever.

Daniel, now changed, sat back on his bed and

listened to the shouting below. Daniel didn't know which was the loudest, the violent thunderclaps outside or the two drunkards in the hallway. He held his head in his hands then suddenly jumped up from his bed, the wrath of his once lovely mother ripped into his eardrums again like the clap of thunder outside.

"Daniel get out of your pit of a bed and make sure you turn the lights off and let that useless mutt of a dog out before you go to school". With that and a loud slam of the front door the storm chasers were gone.

The boy made his way along the freezing landing towards the bathroom. The bathroom was dark and cold, the light blue coloured paint on the walls was mouldy like in all the bedrooms and peeled off in rolls.

Daniel turned on the light and made his way towards the sink. He turned on the tap and placed his hands into the freezing running water. With no sign of any soap, he quickly rinsed his face and looked for the towel which was thrown in a heap by the old cast iron bathtub. Daniel dried his face in the mould smelling bath towel and made his way downstairs towards the kitchen. The state of the kitchen made him heave again. Last night's cold runny egg was now dripping off the plate onto the kitchen floor. Daniel didn't know which was the cleanest, the floor or the draining board. He flicked on the kettle just as his dog Taff, or mutt as his beloved mother had put it, entered the kitchen wagging his small white stumpy tail. Taff was a lovely black and white short-legged terrier that had been given to Daniel's, brother Alan, by a local farmer. Alan was now 23 years old and had moved out of number 38 and lived in a beautiful cottage in the mountains above the village.

Daniel patted Taff on the head as the terrier ran past and started to lick up the runny egg off the floor. Daniel still shivering walked into the living room, turned on the light and sat in front of the dead coal fire. The living room was always dark, cold and gloomy. Whatever possessed the Hawthorns to pick that large dark purple and gold patterned wallpaper Daniel thought to himself.

The weather outside was not letting up and was getting worse by the minute. The wind and rain battered number 38 trying every possible way to enter.

Daniel shivered again and looked up at the battery clock on the living room wall, it read 8.55am.

"Oh no I'm going to be late again" he muttered to himself. He quickly picked up his school jumper off the living room chair and threw it over his head.

Suddenly his nostrils awoke again smelling his sweaty armpit odour as he placed the dark blue jumper over his head. He raced back into the kitchen to turn the kettle off. As he did, he noticed Taff who was now on the draining board gulping down the rest of Mr Hawthorn's mug of tea. The runny egg and toast were now history, Taff had done the best cleaning job number 38 had seen in years.

Daniel turned off all the lights and snatched his school bag and coat from the hall and opened the front door. The wind and rain rushed into number 38 once again, as if it owned it. The door slammed into the hallway wall as Daniel quickly battled against the elements to close it shut behind him. The storm was upon him.

Daniel placed his jacket over his head and stepped out of the porch into the mini hurricane. The garden gate slammed hard three or four times onto the broken latch. Daniel with his skinny arm held open the gate then ran through it onto the Old Black Street Estate road.

Water was gushing down the street like a river. The lights in all the houses flickered on and off as the storm ripped through the small village. The wind caught Daniel's coat and smashed it hard into the deepest puddle in the street. Daniel, soaked to his skin, picked up his drenched coat and started running towards the local village school which was about five minutes away.

Daniel raced up towards the old school passing the mighty oak tree at the top of the road that led to the entrance of the estate.

Huge skinny pine trees in the school grounds danced and bumped into each other like drunkards on a night out in the Highwayman's Arms. Daniel raced into the school grounds and was just about to open the large oak school door when a sarcastic teacher's muffled voice rose above the wind and shouted

"Late again are we Mr Hawthorn"? it was Mr Smith the music teacher or Smitty as the students called him. Smitty's hair was quite long and grey and it had that flick over thing some people have as they get older. Daniel, soaked to the bone, grinned as he held his head in his hands to shelter the wind from his face. Smitty's hair was all over the place, flapping in his face like a flat fish looking as if it wanted to escape off his head. Daniel smirked again as he turned away and held open the door. Smitty with his crazy wet hair frowned and fled passed Daniel like a skinny whippet.

Daniel noticed the music teacher's red-veined skin; it was very similar to his dad's. Whisky, Daniel thought to himself.

Daniel let the heavy door close behind him with a loud crash and started running towards his classroom. It was Monday morning and the school corridor was cold, the boiler had blown out in the night and the whole school was freezing. Daniel hoped he would be sent home but no such luck. Caretaker Jack was on the case. The boiler would soon be back up and running. No job too big or too small for Jack.

Daniel entered form room 9c just as the form teacher Mr Raymond Giles, or Piles as all the students called him, was reading the register. Daniel sneaked towards the back of the classroom to his usual seat by the window hoping Piles hadn't seen him. Suddenly Piles slammed down the register as a clap of thunder shook the room.

"Late again Hawthorn" the angry Piles screamed, "don't you understand that school starts at 9am. Not five past nine, ten past nine, or not even twenty-five past nine its starts at 9am, do you understand? Are your parents daft or what?".

A flash of lightning lit up the dull classroom to reveal another teacher with a road map complexion.

Daniel bowed his head and only wished Piles knew about his home life. As usual, he got afternoon detention. Piles with his smelly garlic rotten breath finished the register and asked Peter Perfect, the teacher's pet to take the register back to the office. Peter took the black registration book from his Master and trotted off out of the classroom. Piles sat at his desk and gazed through his brass coloured half-glasses at his daily paper. The class sat silently and waited.

Daniel looked outside the window and couldn't believe the strength of this almighty storm. Massive branches had been ripped away from the trees and lay in the playground like dead alligators. The trees swayed from side to side like a metronome.

Suddenly the school bell rang. Everybody got up and started making their way towards the door. Piles stood up pointing his finger at his flock and grimaced over his half brass coloured glasses, the students stopped like they had hit a brick wall.

"Sit down", mouthed the controlling garlic smelling Piles, still pointing his finger. Everyone did as they were told and backed up towards their wooden chairs like frightened animals. Piles was indeed in his worst mood ever. Daniel sat back down and gazed at the maniac in front of him.

The classroom light flickered off as a massive clap of thunder shook the classroom. Piles stood in the dark classroom still pointing his long fingers at his students. Daniel gazed at the dark figure in front of him, his nightmare for a second returned and flickered in his mind. The sky outside was nearly as black as night, as Piles told his sheep to slowly make their way towards the first lesson. As they walked past him, he pointed at each and every one of them emphasising his authority. Daniel was the last out of class when Piles grabbed him by his ear.

"Listen boy" threatened stinky breath Piles "you misbehave or be late again this week and you'll be in trouble, and I mean trouble. Do you hear me?".

With that, he clipped Daniel across the back of his head with his newspaper and told him to go to his next lesson. Daniel hated Piles as much as Piles hated him and knew if he didn't run to his next lesson he would be late again, and you didn't want to mess with his next teacher Rottweiler Riley. The boy, gasping for breath just got to the lesson as Davey a lovely lad from the village was closing the door. Daniel entered the room and Riley gazed at him as he slowly walked towards the desk at the back of the classroom.

Daniel sat down feeling Riley's green piercing eyes burning holes into the back of his head.

"Morning my beauties," said the teacher sarcastically, gazing around at her flock like a wolf. The class solemnly replied.

"Page 96 in your books please" she demanded.

Daniel like all the students quickly turned to the correct page. Riley explained that they had half an hour of reading and then they would have a test on the Battle of Hastings.

Daniel looked at his book and then at the much more interesting ever darkening black sky outside.

The clouds were amazing, like massive blooms of smoke bursting out of a volcano. Daniel turned his head and gazed at all the students busy reading ready for their next test.

Lightning lit up the room just as his eyes caught Riley's. Riley manically grinned towards him as she groomed her long wet ginger locks. Daniel quickly turned away.

God, she's scary he thought to himself. He looked outside at the storm again wishing he was on some Spanish island in the sunshine. No chance of that in the Hawthorn family, the nearest Daniel got to have a holiday was a night away at his cousin's farm.

Daniel snuggled up to the radiator beneath the window that was just beginning to get warm.

Jack The Job, job done.

With his head in his hands Daniel slipped off into a daydream of tranquillity, fishing by the local lake. Drifting off further and further into a beautiful sun-filled day catching brown trout by the dozen.

Suddenly his dream was shattered as a three-inch thick history book cracked against the side of the window next to his head. Riley was furious. Her face was scarlet red, and her eyeballs bulged from her frowned expression. She rushed down the classroom aisle as if she was on skies and grabbed Daniel by his collar. The rest of the class gazed in silence. Riley yelled on top of her voice as Daniel shivered with fear.

"What year was the Battle of Hastings, Hawthorn?" Daniel petrified and shivering didn't reply, he didn't know. Riley shook him violently

"Hawthorn you're pathetic," frowned Riley leering over Daniel with her wild evil eyes.

"Get out of my classroom and I don't want to see your horrible face in here again today." Daniel whimpered his way to the classroom door and quietly closed it behind himself.

"Your bag, numbskull" bellowed the ginger demon, grinning as if she won a round in a boxing ring. Daniel returned and picked up his bag from the back of the classroom and hurriedly made his way out of the door once more. As he stood in the corridor Mr Damsworth, the headmaster walked past him and shook his head.

"Trouble again Hawthorn, what shall we do with you. Your parents will be told, and I hope this time things will change." Daniel held his head low and didn't say a word. Damsworth carried on walking, making his way towards the school canteen.

Last term Daniel had been absent from school quite a lot because of his parents. They were always getting up late and on many of these occasions didn't go to work at all. Mrs Hawthorn would tell Daniel to stay home and help her with the cleaning. Daniel hated these days, he hated school as well, but those days at home with Helen and Harold were awful.

"Make me a cup of tea son" Harold would bellow from his broken armchair in the living room.

"Me too darling" the demon wife would snigger cuddling up to her fat overweight slob of a husband. Daniel would hear them giggling in the living room as he mopped the greasy kitchen floor.

Back in the school corridor Daniel bent down and tied his laces on his soaking wet black school shoes. His ear was sore where Piles had twisted it earlier, but Daniel didn't let that upset him, he was used to being picked on. Picked on by his father and picked on by Bobby the fat school bully.

Daniel rose to his feet and listened to the wind outside the school. The storm had intensified and was battering everything in its pathway. Daniel stood silent and listened as every gust of wind shuddered the old school's oak doors. Draughts of air raced in through every nook and cranny and danced down the corridor with not a care in a world. One draught grabbed two pieces of paper that were quietly sitting on the corridor floor which flew past Daniel's head dancing like ballerinas. He watched the couple dance for another ten seconds and then as quickly as it had begun, the honeymoon was over.

Daniel paused for a moment and thought about

his parents. His mind went into overdrive, thinking of the good times they must have had. There weren't many, maybe a couple. Suddenly he paused, a dreadful thought raced into his head.

"Oh no," he gasped to himself. Daniel knew his parents would be home from work at one o' clock for their dinner and in all the commotion of the morning, he hadn't done what he was told to do by his mother. Taff the terrier hadn't been let out and he was alone in the house. The last thing he remembered was his mother shouting "Make sure you put that mutt of a dog out or he'll make a mess". If that was indeed possible in number 38.

Suddenly a bell from Riley's boxing bout rang loudly in his burning ears. The history lesson was over. Daniel turned and got prepared to meet his ginger demon. Perfect Pete came out of the classroom first grinning sarcastically.

"Mrs Riley", Rottweiler to us, "told me to tell you, that she doesn't want to see your pathetic face again today, and to quickly make your way to your next lesson." Perfect Pete grinned again and headed along the cold corridor. Creep! Daniel thought to himself. Daniel lifted his bag and strolled towards his next lesson, which was in classroom 10D, science. His mind ticked loudly still thinking about how he could get home just for ten minutes to let Taff out. As he turned down the long corridor towards class 10D, he bumped into Tim, Daniel's one and only friend in the whole school. In fact, his only friend in the whole wide world, other than Taff that was.

"Hi Dan, good weekend mate?" grinned Tim with a smile on his freckled red face. Tim was the same age as Daniel, but he was so much more intelligent. Tim's dad was a lawyer and worked in the city, his mother was a doctor and was training to be a surgeon. Tim was small for his age; his striking ginger hair was always immaculate, and his clothes were always clean and tidy. Daniel frowned and explained to his mate what had happened that morning, and that he had left Taff in the house. Daniel told Tim that he had a plan, Tim's grin soon turned into a frown.

"What do you mean plan, what you on about?" said Tim quickly walking along the corridor towards his next lesson. Daniel explained again about Taff and his parents coming home for dinner at 1pm.

"Listen," said Daniel, "I've left Taff in the house and I'll have to go and let him out at lunchtime, will you come with me?" Tim declined, there was no way Tim would leave school at lunchtime, it was against the school rules. Daniel grabbed hold of Tim by his shoulders and begged him for his help.

"Please Tim I need you to help me" Daniel begged once more. Tim knew Daniel's parents and didn't want to be caught in number 38 at dinnertime or come to think of it, at any other time. Tim frowned and then grinned slightly as Daniel's expression was so desperate. He nodded and then agreed reluctantly as Daniel started walking towards his next lesson. Daniel looked back at Tim, grinned and held his thumb up in the air.

"See you at twelve" he grinned again knowing his best mate would never let him down. With that, Daniel disappeared into the crowd of desperate children rushing towards their next lessons. As he entered the classroom the teacher, a young science student called Miss Wendy Wensil, stood keenly by the door and smiled. Daniel walked into the science lab and sat by one of the large oak desks. A Bunsen burner flickered on the table, as the student teacher explained that today they were going to be dissecting a rat. Miss Wensil placed the toothed beast on the table in front of Daniels's nose. Daniel felt sick then heaved as he looked at the dead animal he had to dissect. Daniel loved science because he always sat next to Skye, a lovely girl from the local post office. Skye was tall for her age and her long flowing blonde locks looked lovely in his favourite lesson of the week. Daniel didn't like school, but science was always good, maybe because he was sat next to the most beautiful girl he'd ever seen, Skye Sanderson. Daniel stooped over her pretending to be interested in the rat dissection. When the experiment had finished, he sat back down and looked at his watch, 11.45am.

"Only fifteen minutes left" he mumbled to himself. He cleaned up the table and helped Skye remove the rat's corpse before sitting snugly next to his first true love. Skye turned and smiled directly at Daniel just as the bell went for lunch, he smiled back nervously and walked out of the classroom kicking himself for turning a bright shade of scarlet. Before leaving the nearly empty classroom he turned around to see Skye still smiling in his direction, he grinned back and felt a warm glow in his stomach where his hunger usually lay.

Daniel left the science lab, and quickly raced towards Tim's class that was close to the large oak doors leading out of the school. He stood fidgeting impatiently as Tim talked to Mr Ranguard the English teacher. Tim caught Daniel's eye and quickly ended the conversation and walked over towards his best friend. The two boys walked towards the big oak doors as a violent gust of wind roared around the school.

"Ready mate?" grinned Daniel, Tim never said and word and just nodded, he looked petrified. The boys opened the big oak school door and stepped outside into the belly of the violent storm

Chapter 3
Number 38

Daniel, closely followed by Tim, quickly made a run for the school gates as a gust of wind ripped a large branch off one of the massive drunken dancing yew trees missing them by inches.

Suddenly a voice shouted from the teacher's staff room window. It was Davies the grumpy P.E teacher, half munching on his tuna and salad sandwiches.

"Hawthorn, Thompson where on earth do you think you are going?" Still stuffing his face with the rest of his tuna sandwich.

"To get our football sir, yelled Daniel grabbing tightly onto to the school gates as a gust of wind nearly toppled his frail body over.

"Playing football in this weather" yelled Davies "you must be mad, hurry up and get back into school, and Hawthorn put your coat on." Davies quickly closed the staff room window shivered and returned to his healthy lunch.

The two boys, totally not listening to Davies, ran as fast as they could out of the school gates and headed for cover in the old slate roofed bus shelter just outside the school grounds.

"We've made it Tim" grinned Daniel excitedly, looking back at the old school with a drip of rainy snot hanging like string from his nose. Tim stood in the bus shelter and gazed back at the 99-year-old school. The school looked scary in the mid-December storm, the orange street lights were still on and flickered brightly against the jet-black stormy sky.

"We'll be in big trouble if we don't get back before the end of the break" frowned Tim.

"Oh, stop your moaning and come on," replied Daniel, grabbing Tim by the arm "we won't be long."

The boys moved on forwards towards number 38, passing the large ancient oak tree at the entrance of Old Black Street Estate. The old oak had many a tale to tell. Some say it was cursed in the year 1787 by the old black witch of Bont, often seen by the elderly on Halloween. Others said it was just pure evil. Many of the elderly people in the village would say that in the dead of night, especially on Halloween, its large arm-like branches would come alive and if you walked past at a certain time it would grab you into its hollow wide belly, and you would never be seen again.

Tim looked around and gazed back at the ancient tree terrified as all the old folk stories flooded into his brain. The tree's arm-like branches swayed wildly in the wind like a heavyweight boxer, as the storm tried desperately to remove one of them. All Tim wanted to do was to be back in his comfortable warm classroom. Instead, he was bunking off school going to look what Daniel's stupid mutt of a dog had been up too.

Suddenly Daniel yelled. "Quick Tim let's run for it," as the blustering wind ceased for a second. The boys ran as fast as they could. They ran past the old church that had seven candles lit in its massive stained-glass windows. Another thirty yards and they passed Mr Hawthorn's second home the Highwayman's Arms. The street ahead looked more like a river than a road. Finally, Daniel's house was in view as they ran along the tarmac river towards the bottom of Old Black Street Estate. Eventually they arrived at number 38 just as the rain started pouring down again. They raced towards the front door as the storm collected its thoughts and returned, again with a vengeance.

A clap of thunder shuddered the street followed by an almighty flash of lightning. The street lights flickered then went out with a loud bang, suddenly the estate was black. The storm had won its first major contest and had blown the main electricity supply box next to the Highwayman's Arms. Daniel shivered and fumbled around in his sodden school trousers and pulled out his front door key from his pocket. The whole of Black Street was dark and gloomy. Evil felt close-very, very, close.

The large overgrown privet garden hedges had now turned black and danced violently, wanting desperately to rip themselves from their roots and run off to the warmth of sunny Spain.

"Hurry up Dan I'm getting soaked" shouted Tim.

"It won't open," replied Daniel "it's blocked by something."

The boys plus the unwelcomed gush of wind pushed as hard as they could against the jammed front door.

Suddenly the door burst open and the boys fell into a heap on the cold, damp carpet.

"Oh my god" gasped Daniel in disbelief "what has that dog done now" Tim just stood there motionless, rain dripping off his nose like a leaking tap. The scrawny little terrier Taff was nowhere to be seen, but as expected had done his deed for the day.

He had ripped the dark red hall carpet right down its middle while trying to get out of the house.

Now number 38 was not the tidiest house in the world but if the Hawthorns saw what Taff had done, he would be taken to the vets and sent to terrier heaven for sure.

Tim held his nose as the stench of stale beer and chip fat entered his nostrils. The street and house lights flickered on again as the many strips of wallpaper hanging off the walls applauded in the wind like an audience watching a comedian.

"TAFF!!" screamed Daniel at the top of his voice in anger, but the terrier was nowhere to be seen. Tim passed the wallpaper audience and walked into the kitchen.

"Oh no" smirked Tim. Daniel raced down the hall and entered the kitchen and couldn't believe his eyes. The whole kitchen was covered in flour, the floor the walls and even the cooker.

"Taff" screamed Daniel once more but still there was no sign of the little black and white not so innocent terrier.

"Tim, we'll have to clean this mess up before my parents come home for dinner" Tim's smirk soon turned into a sullen frown.

"But what about school?" asked Tim, "Never mind school, if I don't clean up this mess my parents won't let me see you again until I'm at least 65." Tim knew he wasn't lying.

Every dinnertime roughly about one o' clock, Daniel's parents would come home for their daily dose of fatty foods. Usually, Harold would have 5 rashers of bacon, 2 eggs, bread and butter and of course a large mug of tea. Helen roughly the same but in a smaller portion. It was now 12.15pm Forty-five minutes to save Taff's life and, come to think of it, Daniel's as well. They would have to hurry.

Firstly, they started on the kitchen, what a mess, there were little white terrier footprints everywhere, even on the worktops. Tim started to laugh, then apologized

"Sorry Dan but I just can't help thinking of Taff running around the kitchen covered in white flour, it just kills me." Daniel turned around and gave Tim a cheeky smile.

Now unknown to the boys, Taff had been hiding underneath the stairs.

Suddenly a gust of wind ripped open the front door and the little terrier made his great escape. He ran as fast as his little legs would carry him, Daniel quickly raced to the hallway thinking it was his parents and noticed a black and white flash zoom towards the front door. It disappeared down the hallway and out of the garden gate like a jet-propelled rocket exiting number 38, whilst leaving a trail of little white footprints everywhere.

"Taff!!" shouted Daniel while grinning, looking at all the tiny footprints some of which had left skid marks along the red ripped hallway carpet. Tim entered the scene and grinned to himself looking at the little white paw prints but couldn't say a word. He fell onto the hallway floor rolling around in laughter.

"Your dog's mad Dan" he howled to himself holding his stomach tightly with tears of joy dripping from his innocent freckled face. Daniel joined in with the laughter as the two boys rolled around on the carpeted hallway. Finally, the two boys came to their senses and re-entered the kitchen fiasco.

Daniel started cleaning the tabletops and Tim started mopping the floors. After about 10 minutes the two boys put down their cleaning materials and stepped back to look at the work they had done.

"Wow" smiled Daniel, gazing at the newly cleaned kitchen.

"Double wow" grinned Tim, "don't you think it's too clean for number 38?". The two boys keeled over clutching their stomachs with laughter once again. The boys were still grinning when Tim dampened the moment,

"But what about the carpet?"

"Don't worry mate, I have an idea" grinned Daniel.

The boys walked out of the kitchen door and into the overgrown garden. The old cooking apple tree by the garden shed bent in two with the wind, then sprung back and snapped in half like a twig. The boys made their way along the moss-covered path towards Harold's haven, his garden shed.

A large black rat soaked to its skin ran in front of Daniel's feet and disappeared under the garden fence. Harold Hawthorn's shed was his pride and joy. The shed was immaculate, jars of screws lay side by side like soldiers on oak shelves. Screwdrivers sat with hammers, chisels and pliers on their fitted units in the corner. In one corner of the shed was an old comfy armchair where Harold Hawthorn sat and listened to his favourite music. He thought more about his shed than he did about his house.

"Now where is it?" sighed Daniel, looking up at the neat and tidy shelves covered in power tools, and jars full of nuts and bolts.

"It's here somewhere I'm sure."

"What are you looking for Dan?" asked Tim curiously.

"Found it" grinned Daniel reaching up towards the very top shelf, carefully pulling down a large tin of extra strong glue, labelled, INSTANT FIX.

"I hope so" smiled Tim. The boys went back into the house and started to fix the deep red hallway carpet. Now when it comes to fixing things or anything to do with practical skills, Daniel would be top of the class.

"Right Tim, look and learn" smirked the carpet fitter. Tim sat down next to his mate and watched in awe as Daniel set about the task of repairing the ripped red carpet. Tim knew of Daniel's skills because of the go-cart building in his vocational lesson last term, in which he excelled and received a top-grade award.

Daniel went about his job with an air of confidence and a grin upon his face. Firstly, he opened the large instant fix tin with a flat-headed screwdriver. The sickly stench of the glue quickly took away the mouldy smell in number 38. He placed a wallpaper knife into the tin and scooped up a large blob of the tacky brown substance, carefully placing the glue on one edge of the carpet repeating the task on the other piece. He placed the carpet tightly together as Tim concentrated with a look of awe on his freckled pale face.

Daniel stood up and placed both his scruffy black school shoes down on the carpet and stood motionless for two minutes.

"Hey" smiled Daniel "doesn't look that bad, what

do you think? We'll have to start a business together. We'll call it

"Dan and Tim's Fixing Things." Both boys started laughing again as they returned the glue and tools back to Harold's haven. Then their thoughts returned to the mission of finding the crazy dog, Taff.

"Thanks, Tim," grinned Daniel; "I couldn't have done it without you."

"No problem" smiled Tim "now, let's find your crazy dog and get back to school before your parents get home."

Outside the black clouds banged their heads together creating the loudest sound since the dam disaster in Garrog in 1925.

It was now 12.25pm but outside it was pitch black. The power station by the Highwayman's Arms rumbled and roared its way in and out of life. The orange street lights flickered on and off again like candles in the devastating downpour.

The boys left number 38 with a loud slam of the front door. The garden gate slammed shut loudly in the wind. The whole of Old Black Street Estate was deserted, not even a cat was to be seen.

"Where do you think Taff will be?" asked Tim shivering while zipping up his nice new winter's jacket. Daniel, wearing his unzipped broken, green hand me down coat, replied calmly with fear in his voice

"Just follow me." Daniel turned away and spoke no more as he quickly upped his pace and headed back towards the ancient oak. Unknown to Tim, Daniel knew very well where Taff had gone. Taff often went to this place if he got kicked out of the house, but he wasn't telling Tim, not just yet.

Chapter 4
The Mansion

The two boys hurriedly walked up the dimly lit street and headed back towards the ancient oak tree.

A branch reached down and groaned as it touched Tim's head. He quickly moved aside thinking of all the horrible horror stories he had heard from its past.

Next was the Highwayman's Arms, its door locked for a change. The old highwayman sign swayed on its hinges creaking and groaning like an old man's back. The road to the left of the Highwayman's Arms twisted and narrowed on from here and Tim knew they were heading away from the school as the gusts of wind strengthened.

Daniel's hurried pace turned into a gentle trot. The large hedges and high stone walls closed in on the boys like a closing coffin. Tim kept close to his mate as a large crack of forked lightning hit an ageing yew tree right in front of their eyes.

"Watch out," screamed Daniel as the tree crashed to the ground, missing Tim by inches. The boys carried on up the hill and towards the eye of the storm.

"Daniel" screamed Tim holding his hands across

his frozen ears. The wind was deafening.

"Where are we going?" Daniel's grin from earlier in the house had turned into a stare of fear, he never said a word and quickly upped his pace once more.

Tim shivered as he followed his friend, he didn't feel comfortable and he knew something bad was about to happen.

Suddenly the large black hedges turned into ivy-covered ten-foot-tall stone walls. The boys carried on for another two hundred yards when Daniel stopped and gasped for breath. Tim stood next to him breathing heavily and gazed at the horror in front of his eyes. Two humongous black gates in front of the boys stood tall and creaked in the wind. Ivy covered the right gateway like a rash, as Tim stood motionless.

"Daniel" whimpered Tim shivering with fear. Daniel turned and stared again, this time he seemed more like himself. He explained that Taff had been here before in the summer and that he must have come back to the mansion to shelter from the storm. Tim gazed at the gates in front of him, they creaked and groaned as the storm raced through the evil patterned strangely designed gateway. Tim knew of the mansion and had heard of its horrible ghostly stories.

In front of their eyes about a hundred yards along its driveway stood the old mansion. The driveway was covered in trees and brambles and pieces of ripped off branches, some as large as a small car. The drive hadn't been used for years, everyone kept away.

The mansion stood tall and black against the dim grey daylight. Daniel took the first step and heaved open one of the large gates and stepped into his nightmare. The belly laughter from earlier had now long gone. Tim still stood motionless as the gate creaked closed.

"Tim" shouted Daniel above the din of the gusting wind. "Come on."

The freckled-faced posh Timothy Thompson was frozen to the spot. Only once before had Tim ever entered these garden gates and that was in the height of the summer three years earlier with his sister. His sister said she had heard strange noises coming from beneath the ground by the mansion's large oak door. They both stood there as the summer sunshine shone into one of the windows and Tim was sure he saw movement in the window above, yet nobody had lived there for years. The last person to live there was the old gardener Sid The Shovel and he had disappeared without a trace. Tim had run away from the mansion with total fear and promised his sister he would never return. But here he was again with the dread of the mansion deep in his brain.

The mansion with its two large eye-shaped windows gazed at Tim and invited him to enter. Tim shivering with fear awoke from his trance as a branch from an old oak tree crashed against the ten-foot wall. Tim jumped from his coma and shivered once more

"TIM" Yelled Daniel again opening the gate with all his strength. Come on".

"No Daniel please" replied the terrified boy "I can't". The mansion was about to have its first guests for nearly seventy years, and it was hungry. Daniel assured Tim that he would be OK. Tim reluctantly stepped forward as Daniel battled with the gates.

"Hurry Tim I can't hold them much longer." Tim shuffled his scrawny body through the old iron gates just as they slammed closed like a cell door. The mansion groaned with delight in the storm and its victims moved closer towards its massive oak doors.

The terrified boys scrambled through the undergrowth yelling for Taff through the howling wind. Massive brambles grabbed their arms and legs demanding and begging them not to go any further. The mansion lit up with a flash of lightning to reveal its horror as daylight glanced around the blackest cloud in the sky. The two large oval-shaped windows twinkled in the dim light. Bits of broken glass from one of the smashed windows glistened in the undergrowth as ivy gripped the mansion like a knitted scarf.

Earlier that year Billy Buster or Fatso the school bully had bragged that he'd been into the mansion in the summer holidays with his mates and smashed all its windows. Fatso was a liar, of course, he'd thrown one stone then ran as fast he could back towards the village petrified. The Mansion was still looking for revenge for Fatso's smashing behaviour.

The dirty glass oval eyes peered down at the boys who both shivered and took another small step closer and closer towards the massive oak doors. A small wooden slatted fence surrounded the mansion's front garden. Lots of its panels had rotted away. The garden had large black bushes with cabbage-like faces on, they swayed from side to side as if alive. The entrance in front of the two boys had two slate pillars each carved with weird looking creatures of some sort. The garden gate swung in the wind creaking loudly on its rusty pillar hinges. Brambles, ivy and some strange black weed strangled the wooden garden gate but strangely didn't dare touch the slate carved pillars.

The boys pushed their way through and slowly made their way towards the old mansion's dark oak doorway. A strange black rose thorn bush desperately tried to grab Daniel's soaking wet coat warning him not to go any further. Daniel ripped it away as a bolt of lightning lit up the mansion, hitting its highest tower with an almighty crack. They edged along the pathway and finally reached the porch. In front of them stood two large black oak doors. On one door, carved deep into its grain the letter "M" and on the other the letter "H". Carvings of plants and herbs weaved through the letters and seemed to grow through the lettering as the light tricked their eyes. The boys looked at each other not understanding the lettering.

Daniel stepped forward into the porch and slowly tried turning one of the large metal handles. Suddenly he felt a hot burning sensation in his fingers and quickly released his grip. The door was locked firmly, nobody had entered the mansion for years, and nobody would until it wanted them to.

The storm in the valley was now ripping roofs of sheds and houses. The village was locked in a hurricane with no escape.

Daniel and Tim stood in the porch and gazed at the mighty doors in front of their eyes. Daniel, at the top of his voice, yelled again for the tiny dog. But there was still no sign of him, they would somehow have to try to get in. The mansion was ready for its first visitors, it first for a very long time.

Many years ago, Lord Andrew Abersworth had owned the land that the mansion was built on and in the early seventeenth century he'd had the mansion built for his third wife Catherine. His two previous wives had vanished strangely without a trace. His marriage to Catherine, like his previous two was very, very short. Stories told that Abersworth was murdered in the dungeons by Tommy Tallows the mansion's caretaker. Others say it was a witch from the woods by the river, who had put a spell on Abersworth and hid his body in the old oak tree at the top of Old Black Street Estate. Whoever killed him was never caught and his body was not found for months. Abersworth's servants had said that he was a cruel man and that he had died a strange and painful death. Crippled in agony with severe stomach pains and sores on his face that burnt like fire every night at midnight. Two local children playing by the mansion's lake eventually found his cold skinny body floating on the surface like a ghost. His face was twisted in unexplainable agony. Villagers said from that day the mansion was cursed and haunted either by Abersworth or by the river witch.

Daniel gripped the door handle again with his coat then heard a crash inside the mansion's belly. The boys both stepped back from the doorway as the rumble ceased. Tim stood glued to the spot, fear filled his mind and he couldn't move a muscle. Daniel stepped back into the porch and placed his cold wet ear against one of the large oak doors. He listened carefully as the storm roared around him. He could hear faint footsteps inside and trembled as strange thoughts raced through his already overactive brain. Tim unstuck himself from the floor and slowly walked towards the doorway shivering with total fear.

"Wwwwhat is it, Dan?" spoke the petrified Tim. Daniel turned and held up his index finger to his mouth and told Tim to be quiet.

A massive clap of thunder shook the mansion to its core and nearly threw the boys from the porch. Daniel shook himself and knew what he had to do.

"Tim listen, we have to go in, Taff is in there I'm sure."

Tim shook his head nervously as Daniel turned right and made his way out of the porch and down a couple of steps towards one of the mansion's small downstairs windows. The storm hit him again throwing his black greasy hair sideways. Tim stood frozen again, unable to move. Daniel stepped forward and rubbed away the dust and moss from the window. He placed his cold face against the windowpane and peered inside. The room was as black as night and he couldn't see a thing.

Suddenly another flash of lightning lit up the darkened room to reveal its horrors. In one corner of the room tight against the wall stood a massive ebony sideboard. On it stood two strange soldier looking creatures standing side-by-side guarding its dust-covered mirror. A thousand carved small beetle looking creatures rambled over the ebony sideboard's thirteen drawers. On the floor in front of a colossal stone fireplace sat an old rickety rocking chair, the chair moved backwards and forwards by itself as rats ran wildly across the wooden flooring.

Daniel rubbed his cold hands and, petrified, rubbed some more moss off the window and gazed at the opposite end of the room. A second bolt of forked lightning lit the whole mansion like a floodlight as if the storm wanted to show Daniel what was inside. Daniel stepped away in horror and stood motionless at the window. The rain and storm-battered his cold frail body. Inside the mansion's main room on the wall opposite the stone fireplace stood a life-size painting of a man with black eyes, peering black eyes that etched horror onto the boy's already petrified mind. The man in the painting wore a black cloak that hung down to his ankles. In his hand he held a large black wooden staff. The figure stood against a massive snow-covered mountain range accompanied by thirteen black horses. On the horses sat strange weird goblin-like creatures. The weird figures seemed to remove themselves from the painting's oils and glide themselves towards the intruder in the window, guarding their Master with their lives.

Daniel shook his head in shock then turned and gazed at Tim who was still stuck tightly on the porch floor. Daniel stepped back as a gust of wind nearly threw him off his feet.

Suddenly then, like a magician's spell, Daniel disappeared into thin air.

Chapter 5
The Glass Key

"Dan" yelled Tim at the top of his voice gazing at the place where his best mate stood only a second earlier. But Daniel was gone. Tim courageously unstuck himself from the porch floor and moved towards his mate's disappearing act.

"Daniel" screamed Tim again in the howling wind still not knowing where his friend had gone.

Violent gusts of wind threw him from side to side as he fought off the black rose bushes. Tim stood inches from the exact spot where Daniel had disappeared, then suddenly he heard a voice from below his feet. Tim gazed down at the ground and quickly removed some of the thick black undergrowth. The rain dripped off his nose as he gazed at the hole in the ground below his soaking wet feet.

Deep in the hole lying flat on his back was Daniel. He looked up motionless peering towards the black-clouded sky rain which fell heavily onto his shocked pale face. Beneath him were the cellar's rotten double doors which had buckled. Daniel was now inside the mansion and the mansion knew it.

A black cloud above Daniel's head parted and the dark grey daylight sun entered the cellar. Daniel sat up and gazed at the cellar's horrors around him. The cellar was full of old books and stacks of old furniture. A large oak wooden table stood in the middle of the floor of the cellar with lots of strange objects on it. Wooden cupboards lay across one wall like soldiers. Daniel turned his bloodshot eyes to the opposite end of the cellar, as the black clouds took their revenge and the cellar was black once more.

Daniel stood to his feet as his bright blue eyes noticed something glowing dimly in the far corner of the dark cellar. Daniel squinted and tried to focus on the faint orange glow. He took a step forward in the blackness and held his hands out in front of him for balance. He moved slowly and carefully across the cellar's damp floor, the glow getting stronger with every footstep. The terrified boy gazed in awe at what lay in front of him. The orange glow knew someone was near and revealed itself.

In front of Daniel on the floor was a three-foot glass object that looked like a coffin. Etchings of peculiar animals and a large castle lay on its lid.

The glowing ceased for a second then slowly started again. The sides of the glass box where also etched with ivy and strange unearthly plants that seemed to move as the orange light glowed. Daniel's blue eyes glowed orange as the strange glass coffin burst into its strongest glow. The storm outside eased as Tim shouted from the garden above.

"DANIEL." Daniel heard Tim's scream but could not say a word or move a muscle.

The glowing stopped again as if knowing someone or something was close then suddenly burst into life again.

Daniel gasped as something inside the glass coffin

moved. His eyes bulged with fear as he watched the strange object. Transfixed, he gazed at the glass box as if he were under a trance. The thing inside the glass box was hidden by a pure white silk sheet. It juddered again making Daniel jump, but he stepped forward and courageously wiped the dust off the glass box with his trembling wet hand. Daniel's mouth gaped open and then to his horror noticed a hand emerging from underneath the white sheet. The hand was not human, it was dark grey with long sharp fingernails. He gasped again then quickly took a step back and returned to the cellar's entrance.

The daylight parted the black clouds and brightly shone through the cellar like a flashlight. The mansion wanted Daniel to see the creature inside the glass coffin. The rain poured through the hole making Daniel squint as he looked up towards the valley's black sky. He carefully stepped onto the pile of rotten timbers and shouted up to the heavens.

"Tim"

Tim gazed down at his friend as Daniel once more held his finger towards his lips.

"Tim" Daniel spoke softly "you have to come down here, there's something you need to see". The wooden steps down from the cellar's doors had rotted away. Daniel explained to Tim about the glass box and the glowing orange light but didn't dare mention anything about the weird hand that he had seen. He told Tim to find an entrance and get down there as soon as possible. Tim nodded then hurriedly made his way along the front of the mansion turning left around the overgrown pathway.

In front of him stood an old wooden doorway. He tried the handle but like the main doors it was locked tight. He pushed with his shoulder and the rotten door moved off its hinges. He took a step back and charged at it with all his might. Tim, along with the door landed on the floor with an almighty crash. He stood up and rubbed his shoulder as he gazed into the dark room that stood in front of him. The stench of the room raced into his nostrils like a steam train. Tim held his hand over his mouth and heaved.

The daylight shone in and out again from behind the clouds showing the boy the dark sodden kitchen. Old dusty pots and pans lay scattered along the floor like stepping stones. Hundreds of empty tins of cat and dog food lay untidily across the worktops.

Tim, shivering with cold and fear, stepped forward and moved carefully across the kitchen's floor. His nice new trainers stuck to the greasy floor and squelched with every footstep. He slowly moved forward leaving the stench of the kitchen behind him towards the open hallway door and looked deeply into the next room's blackness.

Suddenly he stopped abruptly as a loud crash came from the dark depths. He shivered again but this time not with cold but with total fear. The natural candlelight had disappeared again behind the clouds as a clap of thunder shook the mansion above his head. The room was pitch black, he held out his hands for guidance and made his way towards the doorway. The crashing noise in the next room ceased as he felt for the room's door frame with his cold hands. His eyes slowly adjusted to the darkness as he entered the centre of the mansion's belly. With his heart pounding like a jackhammer he slowly made his way across the large room. To his right, on the wall stood the life-size picture of the man that Daniel had seen through the window earlier. In the darkness Tim hadn't noticed the man's glaring eyes peering at him in the blackness. A loud clap of thunder roared again followed by a dazzling flash of fork lightning. The painting revealed itself to the boy's horror. The man stood as if alive against the mansion's bare red painted wall. His black cloak seemed to move in the picture as the lighting tricked Tim's eyes. The petrified boy looked at the man's eyes, they gazed back at him as if with delight. The light disappeared but Tim knew he was still being watched. With fear dripping from every pore in his body he moved past the now still rocking chair that Daniel had seen moving earlier and towards the next doorway.

A large broken vase lay on the mansion's floor. This must have been the noise he had heard earlier he thought to himself. He slowly stepped over it and made his way forward. Suddenly he heard a muffled voice coming from a doorway to his left. He listened, as the voice grew louder with every footstep. It was Daniel he thought to himself. He moved closer and slowly turned the cold brass door handle. The door creaked loudly as a gust of cold air from the cellar hit his lungs.

"Daniel are you down there?" whispered Tim. Daniel came to the bottom of the cellar's stairs and held his finger up to his mouth. "Shhh." The orange glow lit up the cellar again like a coal fire as Tim took the first step of thirteen into the cellar's cold and damp domain. The thirteen steps were wet and slippery and the wooden cladding on the walls was mouldy and damp. Tim made his way down into the depths of the cellar and stepped off the last step. He looked with wide eyes towards the orange glow in the corner. He then looked at Daniel's face which shone amber like a light at a pelican crossing. The two boys gazed at the glowing glass object not saying a word. Daniel shaking with fear knew he couldn't leave, he wanted to know what was in the glass box.

He took the first step, his body shivered thinking of the hand he had seen earlier. Tim followed closely behind him looking over his shoulder. The glass box shone its brightest yet as the boys approached it. The amber light dimmed then shone brightly again as the storm raced into room. The two boys never spoke a word as Daniel placed his hand onto the glass box. A warm electric sensation entered his frail skinny fingertips. Daniel wiped down the box with his hand and then noticed the silk sheet had covered the wrinkly grey hand he had seen earlier. The first spoken words in that frightful moment entered the glowing room, it was Tim who broke the deathly silence.

"What is it Dan?". Daniel didn't know and didn't know how to reply.

Tim gazed at the object under the silk sheet, the sheet moved again which made Tim jump back in horror. Daniel knelt and looked closer into the glass box. In front of his eyes directly in the middle of the glass case, he noticed a keyhole. He tried to lift the glass lid from its base? but it was shut tight. The object inside tossed and turned around in the large silk sheet. Daniel stood upright and looked across the room.

"We need to find the key"? He muttered to himself. Tim stood frozen to the spot and watched as Daniel paced around the amber lit room. Daniel walked over to an old wardrobe at the opposite side of the cellar and then ripped open its creaky doors. Tins of screws and nails crashed to the floor. Daniel opened all the contents of the wardrobe, tins, boxes, and jars looking for the lock's key. Nothing. He walked over to an old table that sat in the middle of the cellar's wet floor. On the table was a red candle and a large black leather-bound book. He opened the book and saw thousands of what looked like magic spells. He turned the pages slowly as dust filled the amber lighting. He gazed at the many drawings of plants and weird creatures before turning to the last page. He opened the last page, in front of his eyes and filling the whole page he saw a drawing of a large key.

The key was etched with goblins and ghostly spirits. On the top end of the key were the initials "M" and "H" just like the ones he had seen earlier on the large oak doors leading into the mansion. Daniel gazed at the key and wondered what the initials meant. He closed the book with a crash and then coughed loudly as dust particles entered his dry parched throat.

"It's in here somewhere" he said. The boys looked around the room with bullfrog eyes searching for their prize. In the amber lighting, Daniel squinted and then noticed a small shelf above the old wardrobe. He walked over and stretched up to reach the shelf. He pulled down a dust covered wooden box, anxiously he opened it. To his surprise, nothing.

He placed the wooden box back in its place and then accidentally touched a small piece of wood on the far end of the shelf. To his total surprise one of the wooden slats on the cellar's walls opened slowly as if on a timer. His eyes bulged out of his head as the glass key revealed itself. The key was placed neatly on a purple plinth and sat proudly on its perch. The boys looked at each other. The storm had picked up again and the wind tore through the cold damp cellar. The glowing glass box seemed to scream with delight as the key glistened in the orange glow. Daniel raised his trembling hand and pulled away the ice-cold key from its perch. Daniel held it up towards the glowing box and wondered at its beautiful etchings. "M" and "H" glistened as Daniel turned it slowly in his hand.

Daniel walked slowly towards the glass coffin with his eyes transfixed. This was it; the glass coffin was about to reveal the object within. Tim stood close to his friend, as the amber light glowed in their cold wet faces. The boys stood in front of the glass coffin shivering with fear. Daniel, shaking, placed the key into the lock. Immediately the glass key warmed and then seemed to come alive. It turned in the lock by itself without Daniel moving a muscle. The object underneath the silk white cloth turned and rolled with excitement then suddenly came to an abrupt halt. The coffin's lid slowly opened by itself and the object inside revealed itself.

Chapter 6
The Tippling

The lid opened fully as a white haze of mist surrounded the glass coffin, swirling like a mini tornado, then suddenly disappearing like magic in the howling wind. The object now sat upright and didn't move a muscle. The white silk sheet covered its body but then moved as the object underneath breathed heavily. The storm seemed to cease for a second, preparing for the show to begin. The boys stepped back and looked on waiting for their nightmare to appear.

Slowly, like a slithering eel, the silk sheet moved and fell away onto the cold glass coffin. In front of them sat a weird and scary looking creature. It turned its head and faced the boys directly, the boys stepped back again in total fear. The creature frowned and gazed at the boys with its dark black eyes. It sat still for what seemed like an eternity. Then in its strange eerie voice it spoke it first words.

"Do you realize what you have done?" asked the creature. The two boys stood petrified and didn't say a word. The creature removed its hand from under the silk sheet and placed it on the glass case. Its fingers were long grey and skinny. The boys gasped in disbelief as the grey creature leaned forward then snarled and repeated once again.

"I said do you realize what you have done?"

Suddenly like a loud clap of thunder, a crashing noise came from the mansion's attic above their heads. The strange creature looked at the boys, snarling again and showing them its razor white teeth, then quickly raised its head looking directly up at the cellar's ceiling. Its grey wrinkled face grimaced with anticipation. The creature's body was frail and skinny with a black hessian sacking laid over its bony back. It quickly jumped out of its coffin like an athlete doing the high jump in the Olympics and landed on the cellar floor directly in front of Daniel.

The creature stood roughly about three feet tall. It looked up at Daniel directly and repeated its question once again. Daniel shivered but he didn't reply. The creature turned to the coffin and with its wrinkly hand removed an old piece of green Wallem Wood. The piece of wood stood proudly in its owner's hand like a magic wand. The banging in the attic grew louder as the storm above their heads once again came to life and belted against the mansion's slate roof. The creature lifted its head slightly and with its pointed, long ears listened to the sounds coming from above.

"Grotchins" the creature snapped to himself gazing upwards, "They're alive."

The boys looked on as the creature removed a cloth bag from the glass coffin and threw it over its shoulder.

"Your names, quickly", questioned the three-foot-tall goblin-like creature, gazing at Daniel with its pitch-black eyes.

Daniel spoke first and introduced himself, shaking like a leaf. Daniel then explained who Tim was. The creature looked around its surroundings and then thought of his seventy years living on this god-forsaken planet Earth. The banging upstairs was now deafening and quickly brought him back to his senses.

"My name is Zezma," explained the creature proudly, holding tightly onto its rickety wand. "I'm the seventh son of a seventh son from the land of Fentwell. My grandfather was the greatest Tippling ever to walk our lands".

The Tippling stood proud and gazed at the boys. Suddenly from nowhere, racing down the slimy thirteen stairs like a racehorse appeared Taff. Taff ran clumsily into the amber lit cellar and nearly smashed into the Tippling. The creature stepped back as Taff jumped into Daniel's arms. Daniel smiled the first smile of his mansion nightmare. The creature looked on as Daniel explained who Taff was and what they were doing at the mansion in the first place. The creature spoke again looking cautiously at the black and white terrier and explained what the Grotchins were.

"When you placed the glass key into the lock you broke the Master's spell." The creature with its long grey pointed toes moved forward. "The Grotchins are evil."

It spoke angrily. "One bite" it said, and then the Tippling raised his grey hand up towards its throat slowly pulling his finger across it, rolling his eyes gesturing certain death.

The boys looked on not knowing what to say. Grotchins, certain death, Tipplings - what was going on they thought to themselves.

Zezma raised his rickety wand into the air and told the boys to be deathly quiet. The boys were about to have their first taste of Tippling magic, the first of many spells were about to enter this book and Daniel and Tim's lives. The creature spoke loudly as the first spell of this Tippling's tale was cast.

Oh, great staff of Wallem Wood
Show me where the Master stood
Escape we must from Grotchin's hell
A passageway for us please tell

The Tippling, with the glowing amber lit room behind him, stood tall and held out his wand. He repeated the spell three times. The Master's Grotchins had now smashed their way through the attic's wooden floor and were heading towards the large dining room. Zezma cast the spell once again as the evil Grotchins sniffed the air and grew closer and closer. Zezma's eyes turned white and rolled in his head, the first Tippling spell was cast.

Suddenly in front of the boys disbelieving eyes, a wooden panel on the cellar wall opened slowly by itself. The Tippling raced forward and peered inside the dark uninviting passageway covered in thick spider's cobwebs. Zezma removed the first of the spider's sticky traps with his long, grey, pointed fingers. The cobweb traps gripped tightly onto the Tippling's fingers. Zezma quickly removed the web as an enormous black spider the size of a small dinner plate darted along the wall and into the depths of the unlit passageway.

Meanwhile, upstairs in the mansion's large dining room, the three Grotchins sniffed the air again like wolves sniffing out their prey. The Master's picture on the wall seemed to smile deviously in the moonlit room and stared directly towards the cellar. The creatures raced along the dining room floor on all fours and headed straight towards the entrance of the cellar. The Tippling shivered knowing they were close. The boys moved towards the gaping hole in the cellar wall and followed the creature into the depths of the dark, eerie passageway.

Zezma took the first steps into the unknown then quickly removed the goatskin bag he had collected from the glass coffin earlier. The Tippling was about to cast his next spell. The boys looked on as Zezma removed three small items from his small but bottomless bag. He placed three items on the passage floor. The Grotchins were at the top of the stairway and knew the Master's prisoner was close. The first item from the bag wriggled around like a slow worm, Zezma quickly placed the worm-like creature back on top of the other two items, a black and emerald stone and a blue firefly larva. The black greasy slow worm hissed at the Tippling as he raised his dark green rickety wand. The second Tippling spell was cast.

Magic candles on the wall,
Let us see your fireball,
Light the passage, make it bright,
Candlewicks will now ignite.

The Tippling again repeated the spell three times.
Daniel's eyes adjusted to the light and he gazed down
the dark cobwebbed passageway that seemed to go on
for miles. The Tippling chanted again as the wooden
panelling quickly closed tightly behind them. The
passageway was pitch black and freezing cold when
suddenly a flash of blue light lit up the acres of silk
string stretched across the passageway walls. Spiders
of all sizes scampered down the corridor like an
infestation of harvest mice. The gold-coloured
candleholders with their small wax residents lit one by
one revealing the passageway and their only escape
route from the Grotchins.

Zezma smiled at his companions and knew his
magic was strong. The banging and screeching from
behind the wooden panelling was deafening. The
Grotchins were ripping the cellar contents to bits.

Alfren, the eldest Grotchin, was furious. He stood
roughly one foot taller than his Tippling enemy. His
eyes were large oval-shaped and pitch black. His two
assistants scampered around the cellar floor sniffing
the ground like bloodhounds. They knew the Tippling
was close. The Grotchins gave off a terrible smell.
They smelt the same as bullyboy Billy Buster's smelly
stink bombs. Tim held his nose in the panelled
passageway as the Tippling held his finger to his lips

and told his newfound colleagues to be quiet. Alfren with his long-matted hair stood motionless and then gazed around the cellar. He wiped his dark grey sweaty brow and turned towards the glass case. His assistants Donzo and Whizzer snarled again with their razor-sharp pointed teeth as their leader with his long skinny hands picked up the white silk cloth and sniffed it loudly. Donzo and Whizzer looked on at their Master's face. He snapped at them like a rabid dog.

The two Grotchins retreated as Alfren ripped the silk cloth to bits with his razor sharp nails. The amber lit room was now fading quickly into darkness. The daylight outside shone its candlelight on and off through the dark black clouds. The three Grotchins stood next to the cellar's stairs. Alfren's matted greasy hair lay over his face like a scene from a horror movie. He twisted his head and grimaced like a creature possessed. The wind ripped into his face as he snarled once again looking towards his two assistants. Suddenly, he opened his mouth and gave out a deafening scream. He punched the wooden panelling with an almighty blow then hastily made his way up the cellar stairway and back into the mansion's dining room.

Back inside the passageway, the two boys stood petrified, still holding their hands over their ears after the deafening screams. Taff stood motionless and shaking. Zezma knew the Grotchins were not finished and frowned nervously. The boys removed their shaking hands from their burning red ears as the Tippling started to explain what the Grotchins were.

"The Grotchins are the Master's soldiers" he spoke. "They are taller than us Tipplings about four feet tall with claws like razor blades. His voice shook with fear as he continued with his terrifying tale.

"The Master left his dark home on the moon of Dantra about seventy years ago, in search of children's memories". Daniel and Tim listened as the Tippling revealed more of his terrifying tale.

Zezma walked hurriedly down the passageway and continued with his unbelievable story. The boys followed closely in his every footstep. As they made their way along the passageway the candles behind them hissed themselves to death leaving the spiders to return to their dark, black home. Zezma explained to the boys that he had come from a land far away called Fentwell, a beautiful and mythical land full of all kinds of creatures. The Master had made his evil presence known in the land of Fentwell on many occasions, once removing twenty of the children's happy thoughts leaving them sad and helpless. The Master was truly evil. His ageing appearance was only replaced when he stole the happy souls of the young. Daniel frowned as he listened to the Tippling explaining about his terrible tale. He picked up Taff in his arms as they reached the end of the passageway. Two candles shone in Zezma's face as the story unfolded even more.

The Master was at least three hundred years old he said, shivering to mention his name. His skin was a sickly-yellowed white and his long black straight hair reached down to his waist, which always strangely stood still in the wind. Never look into the Master's eyes explained the Tippling. One stare and your happy memories would be ripped from your soul like a thief in a bank vault. The Tippling then explained that he would have to return to his homeland as soon as possible. He knew the Master would return there and was petrified for his younger sister and family's safety.

The Tippling looked up; above his head was a circular trap door. The doorway hadn't been opened for years. Layers of earth and grass above held the door tightly in position. Daniel reached over as one of the candles blew out in the passageway then helped the Tippling push the door with all his might. The trap door's hinge creaked in agony, as the door slowly opened revealing the terrifying storm above. The trap door slammed against the grassy woodland floor as a gust of cold air quickly raced into the secret passageway and blew out the last candle. Zezma heaved himself up into the ranging storm using every muscle in his body. The storm shook his body and nearly toppled him over. The trees in the oak woodland above danced around battling each other like boxers in a heavyweight title fight. Zezma stood tall and gazed around as the fierce storm pushed him from side to side. He then knelt on one knee and offered his hand to his new companions. Tim raised his hand first and Zezma pulled him from the dark tunnel. He then heaved Daniel and Taff onto the woodland floor.

Winter sodden leaves smashed into the trio's faces, slapping them violently and then quickly racing off to find their next victim. Zezma slammed shut the trap door then led the way, walking slowly along the dark woodland, ducking as the branches above tried to hit the intruders. The boys and Taff followed closely as one of the fighters hit the ground with an almighty crash. They all raced towards the edge of the old wood which lay two hundred yards across the field from the local pub, the Highwayman's Arms.

The trio left the fighting arena and quickly moved into a soaking wet muddy field. They upped their pace as the Tippling started running, Taff following on behind as the mud gathered around his middle. The old rusty coloured farm gate opposite the Highwayman's Arms rattled as the wind tried to force it from its latched grip. Overgrown bramble hedges held onto each other for dear life. The gang reached the end of the field and carefully climbed the gate and stood on the cobbled road opposite the pub. Daniel placed his old, hooded jacket over his Tippling friend to hide his strange appearance. The Tippling smiled and nodded, knowing exactly what he was doing.

The Highwayman's lights flickered on and off as a local, Dilwyn Davies, lifted his beer from the table beside the old fireplace. He took a sip then smiled, looking through the small paned windows at the horrendous weather outside. He started to take his second sip just as Zezma passed the window as a gust of wind removed his hood. The drunk's eyes caught Zezma's eyes, time seemed to stand still for a second. Davies's eyes bulged out of his head and shaking with fear he placed his pint of draught ale back onto to table, not quite knowing what he had just seen. Davies never went to the Highwayman's ever again. Davies never drunk alcohol again!

Zezma upped his pace again as they passed the Highwayman's and headed forward towards the entrance to Old Black Street. The Tippling knew his destination was close and raced onwards.

Back at the old mansion, the Grotchins were furious. Alfren raced along the dining room floor on all fours and then raced back up towards the attic. His assistants followed snorting with every footstep. The leader reached the dark attic and ordered his young apprentices to collect his belongings. Donzo saluted his leader and quickly did what was asked. Whizzer the younger Grotchin stumbled around the attic floor looking for scraps of food. His stomach was never full, and he was always getting in trouble with his leader. Donzo handed Alfren, a large leather-skinned bag and a long wooden staff. Alfren nodded his head with thanks and quickly made his way towards the attic's door. Whizzer stumbled across an old tin of rotten cat food and devoured it in one gulp, gagging as the mouldy foul-smelling cat food slumped into his skinny stomach.

Alfren explained that the Master had told him that one day they would awake, and when that day came they must return to Fentwell as soon as possible, bringing the Tippling with them. The Master told Alfren about the secret map which would be hidden in the old oak tree by Black Street Estate. He also explained that they must find it before the Tippling, or they would have to face the consequences when they returned.

Just as Alfren turned to leave the attic the youngest Grotchin heaved and spurted out the contents of his stomach onto the cold wooden floor. Foul-smelling rotten cat food returned to the attics floor, some of it landing straight on Alfren's foot. The eldest Grotchin snarled and hit out at his clumsy cross-eyed accomplice with an almighty blow. Whizzer flew across the attic floor and hit his frail head against the attic's only bit of furniture, an old rickety half-rotten rocking horse. Donzo looked on desperately, he wanted to defend his younger brother but knew his strength was no match for his crazed elder.

"Get up and obey me." screamed the Grotchin.

Whizzer shook his head and stumbled to his feet. His eyes spun around in his head like a Bonfire Night's Catherine Wheel. Donzo held on to his brother's arm and guided him towards the attic door. The attic was now pitch black. The dim daylight that had shone through the landing's big oval window had now gone. The storms clouds had increased again and bumped into each other causing almighty crashes of thunder. The eldest Grotchin snarled at his brothers. Whizzer refocused his eyesight and then hastily made his way forward towards the exit of the pitch-black mansion. Donzo held onto Whizzer's arm and guided him down the stairs following his elder Grotchin. Alfren opened the two large bolts on the mansion's front door. The two massive oak doors swung open, crashing against the mansion's walls. The storm had now won its contest and raced into the building like a bull in a bullring, smashing Alfren in the face.

The Grotchin stood tall in the doorway looking at his surroundings. The large brambles and weeds on the pathway seemed to part like magic, petrified of the creature that stood in front of them. Alfren stepped forward into the storm as it desperately tried with all its might to push him back in. The two Grotchin brothers had now caught Alfren up and stood behind him cowering from the storm's strength. Alfren started upping his pace as he walked along the pathway towards the two large gate barriers. Trees swayed around his head missing him by inches. Not even the trees dared to touch the possessed evil creature from another planet. The Grotchin entered the roadway and then crouched on all fours and ran at full speed towards the old oak.

Now, when Zezma had been placed in his glass coffin by the Master's evil magic he heard him explaining to his Grotchins about the old oak and its special powers and, of course, the map. He was now only one minute away from the oak, one minute away from finding his way home. He suddenly saw the almighty oak dancing in the amber street light. The old oak groaned and creaked louder and louder as the trio plus Zezma drew closer. The storm was back to its strongest and tore down the street ripping a young beech tree from its roots and smashing it violently against a large stone wall. Zezma stood in front of the oak and gazed up at its mass. The tree was enormous and was swaying from one side of the road to the other. Nobody had ever seen a storm like this before in the village of Bont.

The Tippling opened his goat-skinned bag as his friends eagerly looked on. Daniel held onto to his best friend's arm as a gust of wind tried to topple him over. He then noticed his watch it read twelve fifty. Only ten minutes to return to school. His eyes returned to his Tippling friend and knew tomorrow's detention would mean nothing compared to the story that would unfold in the next few hours.

The Tippling drew a silver coin from his bag and placed it carefully on the muddy grass directly in front of the old oak. His long skinny fingers entered the bag again revealing one smaller object. A two-headed tiny snake moved around in the palm of his hand like an eel. Zezma knelt and placed it on top of the silver coin that was now glowing brightly. The coin cast a silver light like a torch beam straight up the tree's middle. The old oak seemed to stop its trance-like dance and groaned even louder. The tiny two-headed snake hissed and spun violently around the silver coin making the silver light even stronger. Zezma told his friends to step back as the rain dripped off his long-pointed nose. He held out his rickety wand with his skinny muscular arm. The Tippling's magic was about to erupt once again.

Tree of acorn and ancient past,
Let me in a spell I cast,
Branches large please show to me,
The hidden map I wish to see.

The chanting of the spell started, but this time with more authority. The tall oak stood still as the storm around it roared louder and louder. The whole street went pitch black as the power station nearby struggled to stay alive again. The silver bright light shone brighter and brighter deep into the tree's veins making it groan and creak in agony. Still, the chanting continued. The amber street lights flickered on and off as the power station tried desperately to survive its near-death experience. Daniel and Tim covered their eyes as the silver light become blinding. The old oak's largest arm moved in defeat and slowly started to move. Zezma continued with his spell saying it faster and faster. The large oak's arm moved like a slithering snake and seemed to point at a small opening close to the centre of the tree. The moving arm ceased as

Zezma cast his last words. The oak's arm struggled to keep pointing in the direction of the small mouse-like hole. One more inch and it would have snapped off like a twig on a young sapling.

The Tippling raced forward and squeezed his skinny hand inside. A mass of wet soggy leaves was retrieved, and he quickly threw them to the ground. The Tippling repeated the process and pulled out a small piece of dampened cloth. As he pulled the cloth from the middle of the tree, the large arm sprung back with an almighty whoosh back to its original position and then the dancing continued. The silver light dimmed as the Tippling grinned then placed the cloth plus the silver coin and the two-headed snakes back into his goat skin bag.

Zezma turned to his friends and explained that they had to return to the mansion as soon as possible. He sensed the Grotchins were close and his next spell had to be cast on the Master's ground. Daniel explained that he knew of a short cut that ran through the old church graveyard. The Tippling nodded in agreement as Tim nervously followed the couple, closely followed by Taff at his feet.

The church in front of them was over four hundred years old and stood proudly against the day's black sky. The storm died for a second as the daylight shone its brightest light over the graveyard, showing up all its soaking wet slimy grey gravestones.

The grass was long and wet and hadn't been cut for years. They entered the spooky scene through a small hole in the church wall at the back of the cemetery. The church stood tall casting its massive shadow over half the graveyard. They slowly made their way through the cemetery grounds then Daniel noticed one gravestone which strangely seemed to draw his attention as the light lit up its sorrowful tale.

R.I.P
Here lie the two lost souls of
Henrietta
And
Harold Huckle
Who passed away suddenly on
October 31st, 1838
Age 27 and 29 years
May God have mercy on their souls.

Daniel stood transfixed gazing at the grey wet gravestone. His mind wandered, taking him back to his early morning nightmare, but still the nightmare was not ready to reveal itself. The gusting wind and storm raised its head again. Leaves ripped themselves off the wet grassy graveyard ground then danced together in the daylight like fairies.

Tim stood next to Daniel and gazed at the gravestone. He then noticed Daniel's eyes which started to roll around in his head like lottery balls in a container. He shook his friend by his shoulders and asked him if he was OK. Daniel didn't reply, his eyes were now bulging gazing directly at the gravestone. A bright flash of lightning lit up the cemetery followed by an almighty crash of thunder. Daniel shook his head and slowly came to his senses, coming round from his weird ordeal. Tim held his friend's arm and guided him deeper into the cemetery grounds. Daniel's legs felt like lead as he desperately tried to move forward. He gazed back at the gravestone with a frown as the light dimmed across the graveyard then carried on.

Zezma knew nothing of the ordeal and raced forward noticing the small church gates in the distance. Two large yew trees next to the gates swayed like windscreen wipers in the gusting wind. Forked lightning lit up the cemetery once again as Daniel, Tim and Taff caught up with their Tippling friend. Zezma opened one the rusty cold metal gates that creaked loudly. He noticed he was back on the cobbled road one hundred yards away from the Highwayman's Arms. They all started walking faster as Tim helped his friend, whose trance-like state was now reducing with every footstep and hurriedly made their way back towards the old mansion.

The large hedges along the old, cobbled road threatened to attack them as the gusting cold wind shook them violently from left to right. The mansion was now in sight as the amber street lights flickered in the strong gusting wind. The Tippling smiled to himself he knew his journey home was now very, very, close.

The Grotchins had now arrived at the old oak not knowing the Tippling had beat them to their prize. They knelt over on all fours gasping for breath. Whizzer coughed loudly as saliva dripped from his grey stinky foul, smelling mouth. Alfren stood to his feet and gazed at the tree with a grimace.

"Give me the Master's map" he spoke directly towards the old oak.

The tree took no notice and danced with the wind, throwing off its leafy clothes in every direction.

The eldest Grotchin grimaced knowing his evil spell was about to be cast and the old oak would feel nothing like the pain that was about to enter its oily sapped veins.

Alfren opened his bag and removed a small glass test tube shaped vessel. Inside the half-filled vessel, a black-tarry liquid swirled around like a whirlpool. The Grotchin grinned and with sweat dripping off his brow bent down and poured two drops of the foul smelling liquid onto the old oak's trunk. The oak continued to dance his stormy dance but then suddenly came to an abrupt halt. Its large arms stood motionless as the wind tried desperately to find its dancing partner. The tarry black liquid raced like eels into the oak's veins. The oak screamed a groan of disbelief as the evil Grotchin chanted its pain ripping magic.

Black tar of Dantra will enter your veins
A horrible death of hurt and pain,
The Master's map you shall show to me,
Your veins will rot for eternity.

The two younger Grotchins joined in with the chanting, standing directly behind their elder brother. The oak, crippled in agony quickly, pointed its largest arm towards the hole in its trunk. Suddenly the remaining leaves on the tree turned black and brittle, then collapsed to the ground in a heap creating a perfect circle around the old oak. The Grotchin's Moon of Dantra's magic was heartless, the tree creaked and groaned in agony as the black tar raced around its veins. Alfren stood tall and grinned deviously then stepped forward. The wind pushed his greasy hair away from his face revealing his sharp teeth. He then placed his long fingernails deep inside the oak's belly. The Grotchin's smile soon turned into a horrifying frown.

"Noooooooooo" screamed Alfren at the top of his voice, his face contorted with anger knowing the map was gone. The two younger Grotchins stepped back knowing their elder would lash out.

"ZEZMA" he screamed as his voice echoed down through the small village of Bont.

The old oak had danced its last dance and started to buckle from its roots. Alfren took a step back as the ancient oak breathed its last breath. The old oak was dead and fell to the ground with an almighty crash, smashing a hundred-year stone wall as it fell. The oaks leaves awoke with the wind and danced around their maker for one last time before flying off into the blackness of this horrible tale.

Alfren frowned again and knew he had to retrieve the map as soon as possible. If Zezma got to the Master before he did, the revenge on him and his brothers would be ruthless. He crouched down on all fours with saliva dripping from his lips and raced back towards the old mansion followed closely by his brothers.

Zezma had now reached the mansion and stood at the doorway. Before Daniel could explain about the bolt of electricity that he had experienced earlier from the door handle, Zezma pushed one of the stones to the right of the doorway, remembering the Master's magic. The doorway burst open and the Tippling and his friends entered the mansion, quickly closing the massive doors behind them. Zezma raced over towards a large oak table and removed the map from his bag. He held his rickety wand in front of him and tapped it three times on the oak table. Suddenly a light appeared on the top of his staff. He placed the map on the table as the storm outside belted out a chorus of thunderclaps. He opened the map carefully, revealing its strange and weird language in the light off the staff. Symbols of creatures, rivers, and rainbows crossed his eyes. Daniel gazed on as Zezma mumbled to himself. Suddenly the Tippling dropped to the floor like a stone while holding his head in his hands. Daniel raced to help his friend to his feet and asked him what the map read. The Tippling looked at his new friends and frowned.

"The Master is leaving Dantra and he is heading back to my homeland.

The Master is going to Fentwell!"

Chapter 7
The Journey to Fentwell

The Tippling knew of the Master's plan and he also knew he was going to try and drain all the Tippling children of their happy memories. He would have to get back to Fentwell before him. He paused for a moment and gazed at a small picture on the wall of the mansion. It was indeed his homeland, the land of Fentwell. The picture was that of an old stone cottage sat in beautiful countryside surrounded by mountains and streams. The sun's rays shone from the sky like flashlights and bounced off the cottage roof. Zezma sighed and hoped nobody had been hurt. He knew his magic had to be strong and knew the Grotchins would come crashing through the mansion's doorway at any second.

The Tippling gathered his strength and turned to his loyal new earth friends and spoke sternly.

"To do this next spell," he explained "we must slow down Earth time".

The boys looked on and then Daniel nodded with agreement. The Tippling placed the map on the floor in front of his long grey feet. He removed his bag from his shoulder and emptied all its contents onto the cold damp floor in front on him.

"Your hair, Daniel please" spoke the nervous Tippling, "I need three strands of human hair."

Daniel held his hand to his head and tugged a handful of his black greasy hair and handed it to the Tippling. Zezma nodded to his friend and removed only three strands and threw the remaining hair to the ground. He carefully placed the three strands of hair on the map. One at the centre next to a river symbol, the second one at the left-hand corner covering a snake, and one on the right-hand side covering a small bonsai tree. The boys and Taff looked on curiously. Zezma reached down on the floor and from the contents of his small bag picked up a small shiny silver sovereign that glistened as the storm's lightning raced into the room of the mansion once again. He rubbed it in his hands and carefully placed it on the last and most beautiful symbol on the delicate map, a pyramid. The pyramid symbol came to life as the silver coin touched its colours. Streams of seven beautiful rainbow lights raced up onto the mansion ceiling. The picture of Huckle on the mansion wall seemed to move in the shadows. Huckle's eyes glared on at the map as Zezma prepared his Tippling magic.

One more ingredient was needed. Zezma rummaged around on the floor and smiled as he held up the last and most important part of his next spell, Fentwell water. The small glass vessel in Zezma's hand was half full of pure Fentwell river water perfect for the time-stopping spell. He held it up and asked his friends if they would join him on his journey as he poured the contents of the vessel over the strange-looking map. The rainbow beams slowly ceased as the boys looked at each other. They knew this couldn't be the end and agreed to go on this amazing but terrifying magical journey. The Tippling grinned knowing his magic was as strong as ever. He then started chanting one of the most powerful and dangerous spells that he had ever attempted.

The time-slowing spell.

Time must stop to take us back,
Human's hair along my sovereign's track,
Fentwell's river water please guide us there,
A spell so strong only Tippling's dare.

Suddenly the rainbow beams started to shine bright again as the Tippling knelt and held his hands up into the air. The chanting increased in speed until the boys couldn't understand what was being said. The three strands of hair on the map twisted together and formed a plait around the silver sovereign as if it was protecting it. The seven coloured beams from the rainbow in the centre started revolving around the room at a slow pace to start. Then suddenly as the chanting continued, the bright rainbow beams spun into a tornado around the oak table.

Zezma looked up and continued to chant, his eyes which were normally pitch black were now as white as snow. The boys plus the agitated Taff looked on as the Tippling placed his head deep into the swirling tornado. The grinning Zezma pulled his head back and told his friends that he was ready. Fentwell was close. His eyes were now back to their normal colour and the Tippling held out his hands for them to join him. Daniel stepped forward first closely followed by Tim and then Taff. The Tippling explained that they must walk into the spell together and to never look behind. The two boys nervously took their first step into the Earth time-stopping spell. The Tippling picked up Taff in his hands and told them all to step forward at the count of three. As the count of three was spoken the boys, Zezma and Taff stepped into the swirling colourful rainbow and entered the spell.

Suddenly the mansion's doors burst open. The Grotchins had arrived but the gang were now deep into their spell. Daniel heard the loud crashing sound behind him and stupidly turned his head into the direction of the mansion's doors. He didn't expect to see what confronted him. A flash of green light burst into his eyeballs like a laser beam. In front of him was now just a face, a horrible, twisted face, the vision of one of Huckle's horrible beasts was upon him snarling with evil, red-blotched eyes. Daniel tried to turn away, but the face held him tightly in its grasp and tried desperately to pull him from the rainbow tornado.

The evil face twisted its head and moved closer then snapped at him with its yellow teeth. Daniel froze and tried desperately to close his eyes, but the face hid under his eyelids, there was no escape. Daniel opened his eyes as the vision moved closer towards his face and was now only inches away. The breath of the beast steamed around the boy's nostrils causing him to vomit. The foul stench made him feel sick again and he desperately tried to move away. The beast was centimetres from his face drooling to eat its prize when suddenly a hand lay tightly onto Daniel's shoulder and grabbed him back into the tornado. The swirling rainbow beams ceased as Zezma looked at his terrified friend. Daniel's eyes bulging with fear held tightly to Zezma as the spell was about to be completed.

"It's OK, keep calm" reassured the smiling Tippling "we're nearly there."

Luckily the beast had gone. The rainbow beams started to disappear as the Tippling and his friends stood huddled together in a beam of white light. Zezma told his friends to close their eyes and counted down slowly from five to one. The Tippling's spell had worked. Zezma grinned as he reached to the number one and the white beam slowly disappeared revealing a beautiful calming and amazing landscape. The trees were huge and danced in the light warm breeze. The mountains above the small valley shone as the snow glistened in the warm inviting sunshine. Daniel thought about the storm that had frozen his bones two minutes earlier and warmed instantly to the beautiful land in front of his eyes. The land of Fentwell had entered his heart. Tim smiled and held Taff in his arms tightly. Taff struggled he couldn't wait to put his wet paws on the warm and neatly grazed grass. The meadows in front of them raced down through the beautiful, wooded valleys and ended perfectly next to a small crystal, clear running stream. The Tippling smiled the biggest smile for at least seventy years. The boys and their new friend ran down the grassland forgetting about all the horrors of five minutes earlier. Taff jumped and spun in the air like a young pup. Suddenly from behind a small mound of grass, a strange voice yelped

"I love it"

The boys looked at each other in total amazement. The Tippling grinned as the voice spoke again

"It's beautiful here I never want to go back".

Daniel and Tim couldn't believe their eyes. The cheeky terrier ran up to his beloved friends panting while looking up with a doggy smile of joy on his face

"It's me" said the now talkative terrier. Zezma turned to his loyal and trustworthy friends and explained that all languages could be understood in Fentwell, even dog language. The two boys grinned as Taff explained and apologized about the carpet. He explained that he hated dog food and loved runny eggs. Everyone laughed including the cheeky terrier.

Zezma, still smiling, pointed his finger in the direction of the snow-capped mountains. He explained that his tiny community lay in the next valley close to the Brittle Mountains of Smor. The boys and Taff looked on into the distance. A beautiful mountain backdrop filled their eyes. The largest mountain reached high up into the sky nearly touching the sun with its snow-capped peak. The warm sun shone brightly into their eyes as they slowly made their way down the valley and into the first of many dark and deep strange woodlands.

Firstly, they had to cross the not so beautiful crystal, clear running stream. They moved on and came upon a rough shale footpath which led directly towards the edge of the stream. The Tippling's smile soon vanished as he started to explain about some of the dangerous creatures that lived in the land of Fentwell. He explained about the Master and the creatures he had brought with him every time he entered his beautiful land. The Tippling grimaced every time he spoke about the Master. He told them about the water beast that lives in the once beautiful river of Asbadan. He told them of the creatures and horrible animals that lived in the woods and on the mountains nearby. The boys stopped smiling and they quickly came back to their senses.

"Don't go too close to the water's edge at any time of the day, especially sunset" explained the anxious Tippling.

The two boys listened carefully as Taff sniffed the air with his tiny terrier nose. The Tippling explained about the creature that Huckle had brought with him last time he came to Fentwell. It lay deep in the once wonderful waters waiting for its next meal. He told them about its crushing teeth and long whipping tail.

"One grasp of the beast named the Isgwitch would mean certain death."

Tim took a step back from the riverbank and stood on the grassy bank next to Daniel. Zezma then spoke of the herbs and plants they must find if they were ever going to defeat the Master. Herbs and plants with powers never seen on earth. He first picked up a small red plant with his fingertips and placed it into his bag. He spoke of the deadly mood shade, a bright purple herb found only by the river's edge. This must only be picked in daylight, he explained, or the magic would be weak and useless. Suddenly, the wind changed direction and the bright blue sky without a cloud in it earlier turned deathly black. The Tippling moved his head firstly to the right then to the left gazing up at the blackening sky above.

"The Master is close" said Zezma looking anxious and scared. Huckle was indeed close and his powers were stronger than ever. The boys shivered as cold wind off the mountains blew forcefully into their faces. The sunlight above disappeared as if a flashlight had been turned off. Two bright red moons in the darkening night sky peeked through the black clouds casting a faint light onto the small valleys below. Zezma leant over and picked a large leaf from a plant called the Firesinth, this was a brilliant and very useful burning plant.

He wrapped the plant's leaf on top of his rickety wand and asked his staff to ignite. The staff obeyed directly, and firelight shone into the darkness. The woodland ahead lay two hundred yards down the dark shale pathway. The Tippling was scared, he knew the boys were aware of the Isgwitch but daren't mention what horrors lay in the woods.

He moved forward as the boys and Taff followed him closely. The stream shone brightly as the firelight reflected on its surface. The woods grew taller and more overpowering with every step. From a distance, they looked small and quite inviting. But now this not so welcoming army of green and brown soldiers were ready for battle. The trees towered above their heads like giants. Zezma picked some more herbs and placed them in the small bag over his shoulder.

Suddenly from the corner of his eye just before the wood's entrance, he noticed the very rare purple mood shade sitting in solitude next to the riverbank. He gazed at the plant knowing of its powers but then his thoughts shivered as the Master's Isgwitch raced into his head. He held his firesinth light towards the purple plant. The plant seemed to move closer, stretching its long roots as it felt the warmth of the Firesinth light. Zezma desperately needed this herb and would do anything in his powers to possess it. He

73

took a step forward off the shale pathway and moved closer towards the grassy riverbank. The whole of Fentwell was now deathly silent and absolutely pitch black. Tim held his friend Taff in his arms as the Tippling held the Firesinth torch closer towards the riverbank. The once warm and inviting stream had now turned into the darkest and scariest river the boys had ever seen. Suddenly the deep waters below started frothing and bubbling violently. Zezma quickly took a step back.

"The Isgwitch" he mumbled to himself.

He picked up some shale and threw it into the depths of the large cold pool. The stream erupted and boiled like a volcano. The Master's beast was hungry and was ready for its first meal in a long time. A Tippling meal would suit his palate quite nicely. The Tippling looked on as the purple flower next to the large black pool glowed in the Firesinth light. The two red moons had now long disappeared as the trees in the woods reached out desperately with their long hairy arms to grab the newcomers in.

Zezma looked on curiously as the pitch black water ceased boiling, turning into a still deep pool once again. He scratched his greasy-looking scalp and pondered on a plan. The purple plant was scarce and Zezma knew this. He had only ever seen the plant once before in his life. That was a long time ago when he first started his Tippling magic. He had been with his uncle and his three cousins Betra, Doelfo, and Zemious. Only Betra and Zezma had survived that horrible black day. The beast had killed his two cousins and uncle within seconds of entering the pools of Fentwell. Ripping them apart with its sharp yellow teeth. That day would stick with him forever.

Suddenly, from nowhere, Taff jumped from Tim's arms like a flash of lightning. He ran as fast as his tiny terrier legs would carry him down the grassy bank and bit tightly on the purple flower's stem. The deep dark pool exploded as the creature raised its terrifying long head from the depths. Daniel and Tim stepped back as the pure white enormous Isgwitch with its deep yellow eyes snapped at them with its razor, sharp teeth. The twenty-foot alligator like creature crawled out of its pit and slithered up the bank towards its lunch. Its long snout snapped again and again like a cell door slamming shut.

Taff crouched down and held tightly onto the Tippling's prize. The beast, luckily for Taff, hadn't noticed the small terrier and edged closer towards the Tippling. Zezma pushed his Firesinth flame right into its eyes as the beast hissed loudly like a rattlesnake. The beast was useless on the ground and moved slowly. Zezma fought it back as the white creature snapped its jaws at Daniel while edging forward. Taff still pulling with all his might on the plant managed to remove it from its stubborn roots. He stood with the purple plant hanging from his mouth but realized he had nowhere to go. The Isgwitch snapped at the flame again missing it by inches. Taff was stuck - if the creature had turned around, he would be dead for sure.

Zezma edged closer tempting it with his long skinny hand. The creature snapped again, this time it was getting too close. Zezma's mind thought hard thinking of any spell that would work just for one minute. Suddenly the spell of sleep raced into his thoughts

"That might work," he said to himself.

He lashed out at the creature with his Firesinth torch once more, hitting it directly on its pale white snout. The creature shook itself as the burning sensation stung its white nose. The Tippling handed his staff to Daniel and quickly opened his goat-skin bag and removed two dry herbs that he had picked earlier. He held them in his hand and crushed them into a thousand pieces. The spell of sickly sleepiness was about to be cast, maybe this would work, he thought.

The Tipping threw the herbs into the Isgwitch's mouth as it tried to snap onto the Firesinth torch in Daniel's hand. The beast engulfed the herbs in seconds, as they raced quickly towards its starving stomach. The Tippling removed the staff from Daniels's hand and held it towards the dark Fentwell skies as the magic chanting began again.

Oh, great animal from the deep,
I cast a spell for you to sleep,
Your belly's full you have had your feast,
Now leave us, go you great white beast.

The creature chewed on the rest of the herbs with his razor sharp teeth snapping and moving slowly towards Zezma. Suddenly its eyes became heavy as the magic herbs ran deep through its veins. Taff looked on, still holding tightly onto the beautiful purple prize. The beast hissed one last time before it collapsed onto the riverbank in a heap. Its large white body lay motionless. Its stomach was tricked into fullness and grumbled loudly then moved up and down like bellows from an old coal fire starter.

The Tippling grinned again; his magic had worked but he also knew that it would only last for sixty-two seconds. The seconds hurried along as Zezma encouraged his friends away from the depths of the deep dark pool. Taff raced up the bank passing the creature within inches. The purple mood shade plant hung from his tiny mouth like a dead rat. Zezma moved up the grassy bank and back up onto the shale pathway. Taff followed on then dropped the purple plant at Zezma's feet. The grinning Tippling picked up the mood shade plant and tapped the terrier on his head. The plant would be a vital ingredient in the defeat of the Master.

The creature moved slightly as the spell slowly faded away, twenty seconds to go and the Isgwitch would be back. The Tippling knew time was running short and hurried the gang along the pathway towards the old wood. Daniel looked back as the creature raised its head in defeat, a horrible screeching howling sound came from its vocal cords. He quickly upped his pace as the Isgwitch lowered his now starving white body back down the grassy bank and into its deep black pool. The grumbling Isgwitch would have to wait for its next meal.

On the pathway, the sky seemed to lighten for a few moments showing them the full horror of the woods ahead. Zezma looked on, knowing what was to come. His days in the woods when he was young were full of happy memories, but now they brought only despair and hopelessness.

They edged on as the woods stood tall and danced in the increasingly bitter cold breeze. The pathway ahead weaved its way directly into the depths of the deep dark wood. Zezma went first and entered the blackness it was if a door had been closed behind him. He looked around cautiously with total fear in his eyes. Daniel sensed the Tippling's fear and stayed close. The woods lay silent as ten thousand creature's eyes looked on, what lay ahead was enough to frighten even the bravest of souls.

Back in the village of Bont, the Grotchins angrily raced along the narrow roadway and back towards the Master's mansion. The storm still held its strength and battered everything in its path. The Highwayman's sign had been ripped off its creaking hinges and lay motionless in the nearby field. Alfren raced in front followed closely by his two younger brothers. The school lights faulted for a second casting it into complete darkness.

The Grotchins continued faster and faster to retrieve the map. The mansion was close and Alfren knew he had to return to Fentwell as soon as possible. The gateway to the mansions drive had been ravaged by the storm. One of the large gates lay on the ground as ivy gripped the spiral bars for dear life. Alfren raced down the pathway smashing anything and everything in his pathway. The mansion's doorway soon stood in the Grotchin's line of sight. Alfren raced down the pathway and smashed the doorway open with one almighty blow. The storm again entered the room as a thousand blustery leaves danced in the eerie dark room.

Alfren stopped and gasped for breath as his Grotchin soldiers stood by the doorway. The elder Grotchin looked around, sniffing the air with his pointed nose. Saliva dripped from his frozen lips and fell onto the floor of the hallway. The room was dark and cold, the creature stood up tall and ordered his brothers to search for the map. They quickly did as they were told and started to rip the room to pieces. Alfren watched on as his soldiers tore the room to shreds. The map lay on the floor next to the fireplace. Leaves hid it from the Grotchins view as the violence erupted.

"Find me that map", screamed Alfren, smashing his fist onto the room's wooden floor with anger.

The leaves on the floor shuddered with fear as a gust of wind lifted them up and they left the room as quickly as they had entered, revealing the location of the map. Alfren took a step forward and reached down for the delicate piece of vital information.

"Fentwell" he murmured to himself.

The Grotchin looked around and ordered his assistants to seal the large oak doors. The storm battled with the Grotchins but, as usual, the Grotchins won. The heavy oak doors slammed shut with a loud bang as Alfren laid the map on the old oak table in the middle of the room. The three Grotchins looked on and knew where they were heading. The Master would be waiting for them and they knew the Master wouldn't be happy. Alfren lifted his wet cloth bag from his shoulder and laid it on the floor. He knelt as his matted hair stroked the oily skin on his grimacing face. He knew his magic would have to be strong, one fatal mistake and the spell would take all three Grotchins into a land of the dead where lost souls, ghouls, demons and witches lay.

Only once had Alfren ever spoken about the land of the dead. Alfren's great grandfather Tesnot had made a potion of herbs and weeds. The first herb was fine but unknown to Tesnot his assistant Noughtos, an old elf from Zentemal, had mistakenly picked a poisonous weed unknown to Tesnot called deathzeenon.

Tesnot cast the spell and the land of demons and witches was upon them. They never returned. Stuck in the land of living death forever.

The Grotchin wiped his oily brow and gazed at the map, the wind had calmed a little outside. He gazed at the hieroglyphics and the pyramid on the delicate map while his brain ticked loudly thinking of which spell to use. The two Grotchins stood by his side and looked on. The storm seemed to cease again, and the cold dark room went deathly quiet.

Alfren nodded to himself and stood up tall, he held his bag in his hand and removed a small round pewter bowl. He placed the bowl carefully on the oak table as a flash of lightning suddenly lit the room followed by a clap of thunder. Alfren leant over and nervously dripped three drops of saliva from his grey oily lips into the small pewter bowl. Donzo and Whizzer were told to do the same. Three drops each no more and no less. The bowl's spit spell of hell was about to be cast but two more ingredients were needed first. Alfren gazed across the dark room looking deeply into its corners. The next item was very important, the larger the better. Whizzer was excellent at finding this item. His long, twisted teeth were perfect. Alfren told his assistant to search the room. The sun shone past the dark clouds and cast some light through one of the large windows into the darkroom.

Whizzer sniffed and snorted in every corner.

Suddenly from under a large oak cupboard covered in carvings appeared the item they desperately needed. A very large hairy black spider nearly as big as a mouse scurried across the oak flooring. The sunlight lit up its back like a torch beam. One millisecond later the spider was hanging from Whizzer's drooling mouth. A Grotchin's favourite meal. The spider's legs hung down from Whizzer's drooling lips like a large Mexican moustache. His stomach grumbled like a cement mixer but he daren't even think of eating this one. His leader would kill him for sure.

He walked over to Alfren and placed it in his hand like a dog would do with a stick. The elder grinned and held the large spider into the dim sunlight then ripped off the first of the spider's legs. The leg moved in his wrinkly, oily hand. He placed it in the bowl of salvia. The leg movement lasted for three seconds then sank to the bottom of the pewter bowl, another seven to go then the final ingredient would have to be added. Alfren completed the leg dismemberment and cast the spider's body into the depths of the darkroom. Whizzer jumped to his feet and caught it in mid-air before it even hit the floor. The Grotchin gulped it down quickly and then grinned, his twisted teeth shone in the sunlight.

The next step was the most dangerous. One mistake and the land of death would pull the three of them into its depths. The elder Grotchin held up his hand and pricked his finger with one of his sharp-pointed fingernails. Black Grotchin blood dripped from his fingertip like a leaking tap. He carefully held his finger over the pewter bowl of saliva and spider legs. He counted as the blood dripped into the spit spell bowl. Ten drops of blood splattered the sides of the bowl, three more to go and then the spell would be cast. The final three drops were the most important. One too many and death land would hit them like a hurricane. One less and the spell would be useless. The final drop of blood bounced off the side of the bowl as Alfren held his breath. The thick black blood balanced on the edge of the pewter bowl then luckily oozed down the side and into the saliva and spider legs froth of magic. The Grotchin's spit spell of hell was about to be cast.

Spitting spell of legs and blood,
Take us on the saliva flood,
A spell so strong with raging seas,
We'll ride the waves with care and ease.

Alfren held both his muscular arms into the air and chanted loudly. The two Grotchin assistants joined in the spitting spell as the storm awoke again and started to batter the old oak doors once more. Alfren held his head up high, gazing at the sunlight flickering and fighting with the clouds. This time the cold winter sun was winning and shone brightly into Alfren's silver face. The black protruding veins in his neck pumped the excited dark blood through his body like a steam train. The spit spell of hell had started. The Grotchins quickened up the spell with a language that became unrecognizable.

Suddenly from nowhere, water smashed through the old windows like waterfalls as the chanting continued. The eldest Grotchin grinned deviously as he felt the magic tinkling through his black blood. The water started pouring down the walls then burst in through the large oak doors and raced towards the Grotchins. The heavy old oak table rose off its feet and spun around in the gushing waters. The winter sun squeezed past the dark black clouds and watched, not missing this show for anything.

Alfren, Whizzer and Donzo held onto the oak stairway as the wind, rain and waves entered the room. The water was thick and gooey and swirled around the room with nowhere to go. It rose higher and higher swirling like a whirlpool. The oak table entered the whirlpool and then suddenly disappeared.

Alfren looked at his soldiers with wide eyes then showed his sharp teeth with a snarl. The spell was ready and the Grotchin's evil whirlpool spun faster and faster with every second. The sun excitedly shone brighter and brighter waiting in anticipation for the next episode of this Grotchin's magic.

Alfren went first and jumped into the depths of the raging whirlpool. His two assistants followed him immediately. The violent waters engulfed the three Grotchins spinning them around as if in a washing machine. Suddenly they all disappeared deep into the depths of the spit spell hell. The spell was complete. The mansion stood still again as the water from the room disappeared as quickly as it had appeared.

The storm outside raged around the now dim sunlit room as the mansion creaked and groaned. The clouds took control again and dulled the fading winter sunshine. The thunder clouds battered each other again shaking the mansion to its core, as the rain battered the broken leaded glass windows.

The Grotchins were now deep inside the whirlpool and were riding the biggest tidal wave they had ever seen. It stood at least a hundred foot in the air; either side of the wave was complete blackness. The death land was close, one false move and the land of death would be upon them. The three Grotchins linked arms and held on tightly to each other. The gooey tidal wave crashed through trees and dark valleys. Two red moons shone deep into their eyes. Alfren shook with fear knowing they were close. The wave rose higher and higher. The old oak table balanced on the wave but then in a flash disappeared over the edge. The Grotchins looked on as the ancient oak table smashed into smithereens in the waves below. Alfren knew this was the most important part of the journey, he was ready to cast the release spell.

Spitting spell of saliva seas,
Cast us down now we beg and plead,
Release us down with guided arm,
Your strength and might do us no harm.

Alfren raised his arm and pointed it towards the land below. The wave rose higher and tested the Grotchin's courage. The Grotchins held on knowing the Master was guiding them. Then slowly the wave began to lose its strength. The tidal wave journey was coming to an end. The Grotchins smiled at each other as the wave grew smaller and smaller.

The mountains around them grew larger with every second as the Grotchins looked on at the valley below. Now above their heads instead of the dim-lit winter sunshine stood two moons which shone brightly into their faces. The Grotchins continued to ride the wave when suddenly about ten foot in the air it did a disappearing act, throwing the Grotchin's heavily onto the Fentwell's soft green meadow. Alfren landed first in a heap by a large oak tree. His two assistants landed next to him with a crash. The elder Grotchin stood up and smiled while holding his hands in the air. The dangerous spit spell of hell was complete.

"FENTWELL", Shouted Alfren at the top of his voice, noticing the deep black clouds in the distance. The spell had indeed worked but the journey to the Master was far from over.

Chapter 8
The Witch of Wallem Wood

Zezma looked on at the pathway ahead, it looked eerie as the trees watched in anticipation waiting for the Tippling's next move. The pathway seemed to sway along the Wallem woodland's floor, as if it was afloat and alive.

Zezma held his Firesinth torch in front of him and took the first step into the deep, dark creepy Wallem Wood. The light shone brightly as the gang slowly moved forward. As they moved closer towards the first of a thousand corners, a strange creature five yards in front of them growled then crawled across the path on its pale, yellow belly. Its piercing red eyes glistened in the Firesinth light.

The creature stopped and snarled showing its long white fangs just like a vampire. Segments of its meal of a hensour snake pig still visible in its blood-red mouth. Zezma stood still as the green and black armoured creature crawled across the pathway and then headed back to its underground home in the depths of the deep dark wood.

Daniel stepped forward alongside his Tippling friend and the journey into the wood continued. Zezma explained about the Master and the powers he had over Fentwell. He explained about the creature they had just seen. It had had once been a friendly four legged armoured herbivore called a Gethian. This creature was once harmless to the Tipplings and the land of Fentwell but the Master had changed that, and now if you crossed its path it would snap your legs in two with its mighty jaws and devour your heart first, followed by your brain. The Master's magic had changed the poor beast into an evil wood demon and luckily it had had its meal for that day.

The pathway in front narrowed for a while as the trees crept in closer and closer. The Wallem Woods were now completely black as the wind lifted and ran along the pathway like a greyhound. Thousands of tiny eyes glistened in the Firesinth light and peered from the wooded floor to the highest trees, watching the intruders. If the Firesinth light went out then the woods and its creatures would take its intruders in a flash.

The trees with their drooping arms grew closer and closer towards the pathway as the Tippling and his friends edged on. The gang pushed their way through the now overgrown path. Tree arms and brambles hung onto their jackets like Velcro trying their best to hold them back.

The two moons above the huge swaying trees battled with the dark clouds to see, but again the black clouds won easily. The pathway was now completely overgrown and only the crunchy shale beneath their feet helped them find their way.

Zezma stopped abruptly and turned his head to one side. He cupped his hand to his ear and then looked along the dark pathway, but he could see nothing. But something was definitely there.

Something all the creatures in Wallem Wood didn't like.

About two hundred yards in front of him he heard faint footsteps slowly walking in their direction. The howling and hissing of all the creatures had ceased, only the wind howled down the pathway racing towards the object in front of him.

The crunching footsteps got louder and louder with every step. Every creature in Wallem Wood seemed to freeze and wait. The woods lay silent. Zezma held his Firesinth torch down close to the ground. The silhouette of the two boys, the Tippling and Taff stood motionless, as the crunching steps got nearer and nearer. Suddenly the footsteps stopped. Zezma held his wrinkled grey finger to his mouth and told everyone to be quiet and stand completely still.

The wind seemed to know that something evil was near and dropped to the quietest it had been that day. The gang waited and waited for what seemed like an eternity. The thick black trees moved in the silent breeze as the object cast a long dark shadow along the shale footpath. The shadow knew someone was there, the shadow seemed large and hunched. What it was, no one knew.

The shadow crunched the shale path once more and edged a little forward. The Tippling and his friends stood motionless as the crunching footsteps got nearer. Suddenly the object spoke.

"Who lies in my wood?", whispered the shadow daintily, holding on to her Wallem Wood walking stick.

The Tippling didn't reply, waiting for more.

"You are welcome here whoever you are" whispered the hunch-backed shadow again.

Zezma took the first step and bravely held the Firesinth torch up in the direction of the shadow. The shadow suddenly dispersed and revealed a small, hunched, very elderly old lady dressed in a long flowing black dress. Her long grey straight hair hung right down her back, nearly touching the ground. Her complexion was pale in the Firesinth torchlight. The old woman spoke again as Taff snarled and the hairs on the back of his neck stood tall.

"My dears, said the old hunch-backed woman holding out a welcoming hand. "You look so cold."

Her grey locks swung in the breeze as the wind grew increasingly colder with her presence. Zezma looked on, he had never seen the lady in the wood before or ever heard of her. Seventy Earth years and things had changed, not for the good he thought to himself.

"You must rest" said the old woman kindly "You all look so tired. My cottage lies deep in the woods, follow me and rest."

The woman turned her back and slowly moved along the pathway. The trees seemed to move aside letting the old lady of Wallem Wood pass with ease. The gang were shattered, and a rest would be a blessing. The old woman walked along the footpath and held out her arm gesturing them to follow.

Daniel felt nervous, as did Tim, but Zezma walked on knowing he needed sleep for his magic to be strong. Taff looked on and didn't like what he saw.

"It's a trap" said Taff quietly, but Zezma needed sleep.

The Tippling moved forward and followed the woman along the pathway deeper and deeper into the dark black wood. The tops of the trees now seemed to touch the sky and the pathway strangely got colder and colder. After about fifteen minutes the old woman turned right onto a tiny grass goat track. She turned and grinned and then explained that it wasn't very far now.

Taff asked Daniel and Tim to turn back but Zezma marched on following the old lady as if in a trance. The unmarked path came to a small stream with mosses growing down either side of its banks. The grey-haired old lady crossed the stream using a small rickety wooden bridge. Her grey sharp fingernails grasped the wooden bridge as if her life depended on it.

"Be careful my dears' said the lady kindly.

Maybe the boys and Taff had got the wrong idea. The lady seemed nice; the lady seemed very nice. A cottage to rest in the middle of Wallem Wood was very welcoming and Zezma started to believe the old woman was just trying to help, which helped him to feel at ease.

Taff knew something was wrong and barked at the top of his voice. Daniel picked him up and held him in his arms. The bark echoed around the valley and then quickly faded into the snowy mountain's above.

Unknown to the wood's intruders the Wallem Witch grimaced and bared her teeth. She hated dogs especially little dogs that barked.

"My first meal," she said quietly to herself licking her lips as she seemed to glide along the pathway holding onto to her walking stick.

They carried along over the bridge as the Firesinth torch lit up an old stone cottage with a rickety thatched roof. One small candle shone brightly in the small circular window in the cottage. The tall black trees danced around in the wind and looked on. The warm orange glow from the candle engulfed the woman's face as she turned around at the doorway and waved her hand inviting the strangers into her home.

The door was made of thick, three-hundred-year-old Wallem Wood that had herbs and elves carved deep into it. The path to the doorway was made of large pieces of slate which the Witch had glided along with ease. Zezma had seen these before in the Fentwell slate mines.

The woman continued to open the door slowly as the glow from the wood fire burnt invitingly into their tired and weary eyes.

"Come in my dears" gestured the woman, once more moving her wrinkly hand backwards and forwards invitingly.

The gang moved forward towards the lovely warm glow, as the cold wind increased, chilling them to their bones. The lady explained there was a violent storm on the way, the biggest storm to ever hit Fentwell and they must rest and stay the night.

Zezma took the first steps into the warm cottage. The smell of broth cooking in a pot on the open fire raced into his nostrils. His three companions followed as the old lady bent down by the fireside and placed a log on the beautiful inviting warm fire.

"Please take a seat" smiled the old woman placing her hand on her back for support as she raised herself from the cottage floor.

The room was lovely and warm. There were three old wooden chairs set neatly together as if knowing that the strangers were coming. The Tippling and his two friends sat down and rested their weary legs. Daniel looked around the cottage as the old lady sat in her comfortable warm armchair. Shelves full of old, leather-bound books surrounded the warm cosy room. Daniel gazed at one that stood out above the rest it read.

"The Myths and Spells of Wallem Wood".

The book of spells was indeed the most visual on the bookshelf. It must have been at least four inches thick and stood proudly next to its dusty neighbours.

"What brings you to Fentwell my dears?" asked the long haired old lady stirring the lovely smelling broth on the open wood fire. The broth entered Taff's taste buds as he sat uneasily on Daniel's knee. Zezma with his tired black eyes explained their story and tried desperately to stay awake.

The old woman's eyes widened as he mentioned the Master but she didn't say a word. She placed four wooden carved bowls next to the fire and started pouring the broth carefully into each one. She handed the first to Zezma who nodded and thanked the old lady.

"My pleasure" grinned the Witch as she handed out the next three bowls.

Daniel held onto his tightly and then placed one onto the floor for Taff. Tim sniffed the beautiful smelling broth and quickly started to devour its contents. Unknown to the boys the woman grimaced and snarled as the terrier started to devour his meal.

The old lady of the wood knew the terrier didn't like her and stood up and carried on with her chores. She watched as the gang hungrily devoured their delicious meals, but she ate not a drop.

The cottage was quiet, only the logs on the fire spoke spitting and cracking as the wind howled outside. Zezma ate his and the warmth of the cottage made him sleepy after his beautiful meal. His eyes were now very heavy, so he closed them for a mere second. A ten-second sleep ended with a start, he had dreamt that the Master was in the cottage eating one of the boys as Taff fought with him violently. He sat up in his chair abruptly as the old lady looked on. "Are you all right Zezma?" asked the Witch.

Zezma nodded as if in a trance not remembering if he had told the old lady his name.

His eyes got heavier and heavier as the Witch explained that she had lived in the dark wood for two hundred Tippling years and that her name was Wallem Wister. Zezma had lived in Fentwell for sixty-five Tippling years and had never heard of this woman before. His senses smelt trouble, but his aching bones needed sleep, only one hour and he would be fine.

Wallem Wister offered more broth and the gang accepted once again. Daniel started to relax and told the lady about life on the planet Earth. She listened carefully as Taff moved closer towards the fire. Tim sat in his seat and started to drift off into a lovely warm cosy dream. Zezma made himself comfortable and listened to the Earth boy's stories.

The wind outside was listening as well, knowing that this night was going to be a night like no other. The storm in Fentwell was brewing as a clap of thunder from the Brittle Mountains of Smor faintly rumbled in the distance. The old woman stood quietly and closed the cottage's hessian curtains. She returned to her chair and watched her four strangers slowly drift off into their drugged broth dreams.

Taff tried desperately to stay awake then growled as the old Wallem Witch grinned at him with wide-open evil eyes. The fire's embers glowed dimly in the lovely warm cottage. Within five minutes all three were fast asleep. The Witch of Wallem Wood sat in her chair twiddling her wrinkled fingers, gazing at her sleeping prizes. Her face had now turned sour. She gazed at her enemies and snarled. The fire cracked as its last bit of life slowly drifted away. The Wallem Witch stood and walked over towards Daniel and then held out her claw-like hands and whispered.

"Earth boy" She snarled "Think you can save Zezma do you, with your pathetic stories about your useless planet?"

She glided across the room with her feet not touching the ground. She peered with evil dark eyes through the hessian curtains as one of the Fentwell's moons quickly hid behind a black cloud.

"The Master will be pleased with me" she cackled to herself.

She stepped back towards the fireside and sat in her nice cosy chair. Her hands rummaged around with her hair as she started placing it into a plait. Her true complexion now slowly started to appear. The horror of the Witch from Wallem Wood had indeed entered the room. The boys and Taff were right, the lovely caring old lady had vanished just as quickly as she had appeared.

The Witch sharpened her nails on the stone fireplace. The scratching was loud, but the gang had been put under the Witch's strong broth spell. The broth bubbled in its cauldron as if alive revealing all kinds of dead creatures. The old Witch looked on as her prisoners lay fast asleep, five more minutes to wait for the broth to fully enter her victims' bloodstreams she thought to herself. Then, and only then, could she eat them safely.

She rubbed her hands together with anticipation, waiting patiently for her meal. Zezma had fallen into a dream of horses and Tipplings. He stood with his sister next to the great river of Asbadon. The sun shone brightly as he danced and played with his sister and his cousins by the beautiful emerald waters of Fentwell.

The Wallem Witch licked her lips and looked on at her meals, only sixty seconds to go and the story of the Tippling Tales would be dead for sure.

No more Tipplings, no more Daniel, Tim or Taff and no more about the evil Master Huckle.

The two red moons of Fentwell awoke and broke free from the clouds for a second. The red moonlight shone through a gap in the curtains in the now not so lovely little cottage. The horror they saw made them quickly return behind their friends the clouds. The witch was ready, and the witch was desperate to eat her meal and return to the moon of Dantra where Master Huckle had lived for a thousand years.

The Witch was once one of the Master's prized assistants. He had brought her to Fentwell to guard and protect the woods from the Tipplings. He had renamed the wood after her and told her to guard it with her life. If she killed at least three of the Master's enemies she could return to his land and he would make her his queen.

The Witch waited patiently as the seconds ticked away in the quiet warm cottage. Twenty seconds and it would all be over. Wallem Wister stood to her feet and licked her lips with the thought of not only hunger but the prize that awaited her. She floated up into the air hovering above Zezma like a vampire bat. Her teeth gnashed together excitedly.

The Tippling Tales were about to come to an end when suddenly Zezma's beautiful dream was broken. Unbeknown to the Witch, the Tipplings had an incredible awareness of danger when dreaming. In his dream, he was sat next to his cousin and sister by the beautiful emerald river of Asbadan. Suddenly his sister Helta turned to him and shouted for him to awake. The Tippling looked at her as the clock ticked closer towards his death. His cousin shook him violently in his dream and told him to return to the Witch's cottage.

Zezma moved awkwardly in his chair by the fire in the cottage as the Witch prepared to devour one of the Master's worst enemies. The Wallem Witch was ready, ten seconds and counting. Nine, eight, seven, six.

Zezma rummaged in his chair with his sister screaming in his ear to awake. Wallem Wister opened her mouth wide ready to take her first bite. Black slimy saliva dripped from the corner of her mouth and landed on the Tippling's face. Her arms opened wide ready for her feast. Helta quickly pushed her brother into the cold stream. Five, four, three, two, one. Zezma awoke abruptly and saw the horror of the Witch hovering above him. Her teeth gnashing open and closed like a shredding machine. He jumped to his feet with one second of the death clock left.

The two red moons shone their brightest and tried to peek through the hessian curtains waiting to see what happened next. Zezma grabbed the Witch with his entire strength and threw her against the fireside wall. She bounced off the wall like a spring and returned in a flash. She was hungry not only for flesh but for the journey back to her Master and the moon of Dantra. She desperately wanted to be the next Queen of Dantra, and no one was going to stop her.

The two boys and Taff still slept soundly in their broth drugged dreams. The room had now gone a deathly cold as the Witch returned a blow, hitting Zezma straight off his feet landing him on the floor with a heavy thud

"YOU"RE MINE" snapped the Witch, scratching the Tippling along his grey face as blood gushed onto the stone floor.

"YOU'RE ALL MINE" repeated the Witch scratching and screaming at the Tippling.

Zezma quickly rose to his feet, as cold breath spurted from his mouth and almost froze. The Witch raised her hand and cast a bolt of lightning straight across the room, stunning the freezing Tippling. The two moons shone brightly through the gap in the curtains and gazed at the horror inside the cottage. Zezma shook himself and quickly pulled some Firesinth plants from his cloth bag and threw them on to the dead fire. One faint amber log gripped the plant then lit itself and the room burst into a bright orange glow.

The Witch stepped back and knew she had a battle on her hands. She quickly glided up onto the ceiling and hung upside down like a bat. Zezma picked up his rickety staff from the cold cottage floor and cast a bolt of lightning directly at the Witch. It missed her by inches and left a large burnt indentation on the wall. Wallem hissed and snapped her teeth once more.

The battle continued as the boys and Taff still slept soundly. The room warmed up quickly as the Firesinth plants burnt brightly. The storm was ceasing as the two red moons looked on in anticipation waiting to see who would win that night's main event.

The Witch moved from corner to corner gliding in thin air. Zezma tried to hit her again with his staff but she was too quick. Suddenly a flash of bright light burst into the room almost blinding the Tippling. He closed his eyes in agony as the Witch stopped dead in her tracks. Zezma opened his eyes to a deathly sight. On the wall above the fireplace an apparition had appeared, it was the Master. His face was contorted and snarled evilly at Zezma.

"DEATH TO ALL THE TIPLINGS AND THOSE WHO HELP THEM"

Zezma stood stunned and motionless as the Witch looked on in awe. Wallem knelt in front of her Master and looked up, her plaited hair lay long down her back like a snake. She held out her arms widely and asked the Master for his love. This was Zezma's only chance.

He picked up his staff to cast a deadly Tippling spell called the fire snapper. This spell called for great strength and had only been done by Zezma once before. This spell took four seconds to explode and the subject had to be totally still for it to work correctly.

The Wallem Witch was in awe, gazing up at her

beloved Master and forgetting about her battle with the Tippling. The thought of being the Queen of Dantra had weakened her senses. Zezma pulled the rest of the Firesinth from his cloth bag and along with the snapper plant placed it quickly onto the tip of his staff. He pointed his staff into the direction of his enemy.

The Master looked on desperately willing for his Witch to return to the fight. The Tippling held his staff proudly and sent the terrifying spell directly towards the back of the Witch's head. The spell left the tip of his rickety staff like a rocket, lighting up the room like a floodlight. The fire snapper spell was cast, as the Tippling's chanting begun

Wallem Witch of Wallem wood,
Your evil deeds are deemed no good,
A fire of hell is cast on you,
A Tippling spell that's strong and true.

The light hit the Wallem witch directly in the back of her head. Her body instantly burst into flames. Crippled in agony and screaming the witch gazed up at her beloved groom that was never going to be. The fire snapper had worked. Zezma repeated the spell, his voice slurring as he did so.

The witch stood up screaming at the top of her voice.

"Nooooooo"

She wriggled and tried desperately to reach her enemy, but it was too late. She collapsed to the stone floor in a heap and the broth spell vanished with her agonizing death. Suddenly Daniel awoke. His eyes bulged with fear noticing the Witch burning in front of his eyes. Tim and Taff awoke seconds later, gazing at the horror in front of them. The old woman of the wood was now just a pile of grey dust. Particles flew around the room in the fire light. Wallem Wister was dead.

The apparition of the Master had vanished as quickly as it appeared. Huckle's visit to the Witch was not a good one and he knew he would have a fight on his hands.

Zezma fell heavily onto the cottage floor. The spell had completely zapped him of his energy. He held his bruised and bloodied body as Daniel helped him to his feet. The Tippling explained about the Witch and what had happened. The gang stood together and gazed at the Firesinth fire, realizing how lucky they were to be alive.

The two moons outside shone brightly after watching that night's main event. What else could happen on that cold and evil night? No one knew, no one even dared to imagine.

Chapter 9
The Guardian of the Gate

Daniel stood next to Zezma as the remains of Witch's dust particles floated around the small cottage like fairies. The Tippling was exhausted and sat next to the fireside. His breathing was shallow as Tim brought him a glass of water from the cottage's kitchen.

The Tippling smiled at his friend and slowly sipped the cold refreshing Fentwell water. He reached into his cloth bag and placed a large brown Fentwell healing leaf on his sweaty brow. The healing leaf relaxed his body and calmed down his pumping heart. Sweat poured from his face as the fire warmed his body.

Zezma looked around the cottage with his drooping-tired eyes and knew he had to explore the Witch's treasures. The Master's apparition on the wall earlier had revealed Zezma and his friends to Huckle. Zezma knew it wouldn't be long before they would meet and the Master's magic was much stronger than his own.

Zezma slowly rose to his feet and started to rummage around the room looking for anything that he could use for his magic spells. The first thing that caught his eye was the great book of Myths and Spells of Wallem Wood that sat neatly next to its neighbours on the old dusty oak bookshelf. The book moved forward by itself wanting the Tippling to pick it up to reveal all its spells and potions inside.

He reached up and carefully pulled it from the bookshelf as the book jumped excitedly into his hand. A small bright red spider sitting on the bookshelf peered its black eyes at the Tippling and then scurried along the shelf and dangled from its web in mid-air.

Zezma placed the book on the cottage's Wallem wood tabletop. The book was covered in cobwebs and dust and sat patiently waiting for its next spell to used. Zezma opened the large book's cover and revealed its first page. It was immaculate, just like the first day it had been made. The Brittle Mountains of Smor covered the page looking like Everest and the two moons looked real and gleamed off the page like two dishwasher clean dinner plates.

Zezma smiled, this was Fentwell hundreds of years previously. He gazed at the beautiful scene in front of his eyes. The stream of Asbadon wound down the valley as beautiful green trees stood tall next to their energy source. The gang looked on in awe.

Suddenly a bright light lit up the room as the book came alive, its first journey of many was just about to begin. The scene from its first page was now projected into the room. The two red moons from the book glowed from the ceiling into the room as a warm breeze from the partially opened window floated around like a ghost. The valley was alive and now entered the depths of the small cottage.

The slate cottage floor had turned to luscious green meadows. Trees in the corner of the cottage danced in the breeze like angels. Daniel felt warmth and happiness and knew Zezma was pleased. The vision lasted for twenty seconds and then slowly and calmly vanished back onto the paper. The room was back as it was earlier.

The small pile of the Witch's dust lay on the floor in front of the fire. It seemed the book's next journey would have to wait as it slammed its cover shut by itself with a crash.

Zezma tried to open the mighty book once more but the book of myths and spells was having none of it and refused to be opened. Zezma lifted the heavy book off the table and tried to fit it into his cloth bag. The book was large and clumsy, as he struggled to fit it in neatly. The book was indeed on its journey and seemed to have a mind of its own. It became instantly warm then shuddered violently in the Tippling's hand and shrunk into the size of a matchbox.

Zezma grinned and held the book tightly in his grey warm hand. He placed the mighty book carefully into the bottom of his Tippling cloth bag and had a strong feeling that the book was going to help them on their journey to find the Master.

Zezma continued to look around the cottage searching for items of use. A small green glass vessel sat on the windowsill and glistened in the two Fentwell moons' powerful light.

The storm outside had ceased and the sky had cleared revealing billions of tiny stars.

The Tippling picked up the vessel and looked at the swirling liquid inside. He didn't know what the liquid was but placed it in his bag. The two boys and Taff watched as the Tippling continued looking. Finally, Zezma finished his search and explained they must quickly move on.

The boys nodded in agreement and moved closer towards the cottage door. As they moved away from the fireside and without any reason or knowing, Daniel picked up a handful of the Witch's remaining dust. He placed the dust particles into his pocket which suddenly tingled in his fingertips. No one saw him do this and Daniel didn't even realize what he had just done. The Master was getting closer by the minute, Zezma could feel it. The magic and the spells were going to get stronger. The journey continued.

Alfren, Whizzer and Donzo ran as fast as their legs would carry them. A Grotchin in full flight was as graceful as a greyhound. The three crossed the green meadows of Fentwell with ease. Not like the Tippling and his friends. The wood was nearing, as was the Master. Alfren knew he would have to face the consequences when he met Huckle, but he still carried on, loyal until the very end.

The creatures slowed down as the meadow turned into wood. They stopped and rose from their all fours. They noticed the blackened sky above the Wallem Wood and took a long drink from the cold running Asbadon stream. Alfren didn't say a word then stood up and walked upright into the depths of the wood. He turned and saw the bright blue sky disappear into blackness.

The Grotchins with their amazing night vision didn't need Firesinth to light their way in the dark, and quickly upped their pace through the tall thick trees. The pathway was the same as when they had left seventy years earlier. Alfren knew the wood well and carried on with ease. His loyal servants followed closely behind. The two bright red moons looked down from their perch and saw the three silhouettes moving quickly through the woods.

The cottage grew closer as the wind blustered in the trio's faces. Alfren crouched on all fours again and upped his pace as the pathway widened. The two moons froze and watched the creatures in motion. Alfren's pace was phenomenal at full speed, the shale of the pathway shot up from his sharp claws like bullets. Whizzer and Donzo struggled to keep up with him. The cottage was racing nearer and nearer. The elder slowed a little as his two assistants struggled to catch up.

The Wallem Witch's cottage lay in the wood around the next corner. Was this going to be it? Were the Grotchins coming in for the kill? Was this going to be the end of the Tippling and his friends? They galloped closer towards the cottage, suddenly the corner was upon them in a flash.

Alfren slowed to a stop then raised his sweaty brow and sniffed the air. He could smell the scent of Zezma and growled, knowing the Tippling was close. He thumped his clawed right fist into his left palm in frustration, he knew he was close but had no time to look. His hair stuck up on his back like a vicious dog. He knew the Master was waiting and he knew the Master was angry. Any more delays and he would be dead for sure.

He sniffed the air again and growled loudly. The cottage lay hidden five hundred yards deep in the woods as the Grotchins passed it in a blink of an eye. They moved forward along the shale path. Alfren knew Zezma was somewhere close and snarled to himself.

"My time will come Tippling" he grimaced.

The Wallem Wood gradually thinned and opened again into some more soft meadow fields. The green meadow beneath them caressed their tired feet. The two red moons shone brightly and looked down on the eerie black creatures. Their backs glistened in the red moonlit night. The stars twinkled between the clouds like Christmas lights as they flickered in the night's sky. The wind eased a little as the Grotchin's moved forward.

Alfren's mind shivered in fear as he ran across the beautiful green meadow. What will the Master do to me he thought to himself? His imagination raced through his tired brain. The memories of previous servant's failures scared him.

The Wallem Wood's trees lay still for a while as their dancing ceased. Within the hour the storm would be back with a vengeance and this time the dancing trees would grip onto the ground for dear life. A storm Fentwell had never seen before.

Alfren shook himself and came to his senses, he upped his pace once again and moved forward towards the Brittle Mountains of Smor. The two moons once again glistened but then hid beneath the darkening clouds. In the distance, further down the valley, the clouds swirled and turned violently in the darkening skies like a whirlpool. This was not a good sign; this was like the end of the world. The Master was preparing to return to Fentwell and this time the Tipplings were going to pay.

The Master knew the Tipplings had some strong spells, even some that he had never heard of, but he believed his magic was much stronger and far more powerful.

Huckle sat alone gazing at a map of the Brittle Mountains of Smor and thought about the children's memories that he would devour the next day. His frown was long as he twisted his long black hair in his immaculate clean white hands. His fingernails shone black in his candlelit room and reflected a spider tattoo on his left wrist. He twisted his hair again as he gazed deep into the Fentwell map.

His mind turned towards his three Grotchin's who had let him down. They were going to pay but how only the Master knew. The candlelight shone deep into the Master's mind, and soon gave him his wicked and evil answer, he grinned a devilish grin to himself. The Grotchin's fate was set.

Back at the cottage Zezma slowly walked towards the door still looking around for potions. He could sense the Master was close but never said a word to the boys. He had heard the growling Grotchins from the depths of the Wallem Wood earlier and shivered. He had heard that growling before and knew the battle was soon going to be upon them.

He opened the door and gazed at the night's sky. The red moons looked upon him like two large friendly eyes and a billion stars once again twinkled in the silent wood.

The gang moved away from the warmth of the cottage and headed back along the pathway towards the lush green meadow. The Tippling shuddered holding his nose at the stench of the Grotchins as they walked along the moonlit path. Daniel smelt their presence as well but never whispered a word.

Taff sniffed the ground and sensed danger.

The gang finally reached the edge of the wood. A long winding meadow appeared before them shadowed by a large mountain range. They moved forward as the emerald river of Asbadan glistened in the starlight. The whole of Fentwell was deathly quiet, not even the night's animals dared to scream a word.

They all seemed to know that evil was close. The open meadow soon came to an end as the first of four hills stood before them. The first hill was easy, the second a little more demanding. The third and fourth were difficult but nothing compared to the Brittle Mountains that peered above them in the distance.

The gang moved and scrambled up to the top of the hill where Zezma stopped and gazed at the beautiful sight in front of his eyes. The boys and Taff all panted as they quickly caught their breath. They stood and gazed at the magnificent sight below. It was Zezma's home, the beautiful city of Smor, they had finally made it. With the help of his new Earth friends, he had finally arrived back home.

The city in front of them lay in a small valley at the base of the Brittle Mountains. Small lights flickered in the wood and mud houses just like the stars up above. A large wooden fifteen-foot fence surrounded the city. Around forty Tippling families populated the city of Smor.

The snowy Brittle Mountains of Smor stood proudly above the city like the Himalayan Mountains. Zezma grinned at his friends, his thoughts about the Master had vanished for a few seconds. This was the happiest he had been for a long time. The cold wind off the mountains suddenly increased and brought the

Tippling back to his senses.

Zezma shivered as did the boys, the trees at the edge of the river of Asbadan started dancing and weaving together like lovers. The storm had returned, even it didn't like the feeling of evil which had entered the valley.

The steep path down towards the valley was treacherous, one false step would mean certain death for sure. Zezma went first and the gang followed along carefully. The footpath crumbled away with every footstep.

When they finally reached halfway down the mountain Daniel noticed in the distance a massive pair of wooden gates, the entrance to the small city. The fencing and the gates had been erected many years before to protect the Tipplings from intruders. This land was once peaceful and beautiful, but the Master had put a stop to that many years ago.

Their journey continued as the gates grew closer. The storm had raised its head again and dandruff snowflakes carried in the wind gently fell onto the Fentwell ground. Zezma had never seen snow at this time of year and carefully helped his friends to the bottom of the mountain. Daniel gazed across the valley and stared at the large gates. What lay behind those gates, he thought to himself?

The snow flurried around their heads and soon turned into light damp rain. The wind blew strongly into Taff's face as he led the way towards the city. The gang edged forward as the gates became increasingly larger. The fence walls were huge. What were the Tipplings so scared of? What was so frightening? Suddenly from nowhere, a deafening voice echoed into the valley.

"Who goes there" spoke the voice sternly.

In front of them, appearing just like magic, stood the Guardian of the gate. He stood at least eight-foot-tall and had the biggest hands you had ever seen. His clothing lay across his massive physique like a king-sized bed sheet. In his right hand, he held a large staff and stood proudly in front of his fortress gates.

"WELL?" spoke the guardian once more.

He slammed his staff into the Fentwell ground and stood directly in front of the intruders. Wet sludgy rain dripped off his wrinkled nose. Taff raised his tiny head and gazed at the creature. Zezma stepped forward as Tim cowered behind Daniel.

"I am Zezma the seventh son of the seventh son of Zantor the greatest Tippling to have ever lived in this land".

The Guardian frowned and gazed at his intruder once more.

"LEAVE NOW" commanded the Guardian. "Zezma is no more, the Master took him years ago and he will never return".

Zezma stood forward again and gazed up at the huge bulk of a creature in front of him. The Guardian stepped forward and held his staff up high and confronted the proud Tippling.

"If you are who you say you are you will know my name" said the giant. The Tippling grinned and held up his staff and bellowed out the words into the small beautiful valley.

"YOU ARE THE GREAT GIANT HERRIF HACKLER FROM THE VILLAGE OF HENDERTHRON."

The Guardian stepped back and gazed at the figure beneath him. He peered at Zezma as his mind slowly ticked like a loud grandfather clock. Ten thousand days and nights crossed his large brow then suddenly he knelt on one knee and bowed his head and spoke quietly.

"My greatest apologies Zezma we all thought you were dead. The Master took you all those years ago".

The Tippling told the Guardian to stand up and quickly explained about his long and dangerous journey. He then introduced his friends one by one. Herrif bowed again as Taff wagged his tail. The Guardian lifted the small black and white terrier in his hands and patted his head while holding him close to his chest. Taff for the first time on this strange journey felt safe. Taff giggled to himself as Herrif sniffed him with his massive flat nose.

"You must be exhausted?" said the giant in his deep husky voice, still patting Taff with his colossal palm. The Guardian offered them a place to rest and eat as they all made their way towards Herrif's home which was situated to the right-hand side of the city's large wooden gates. The front door was at least eight-foot-tall and towered above Zezma and the boys' heads.

Herrif bent his head a little as he proudly entered his cosy warm home. His hair was long and shaggy and brushed the doorway as he entered. The wooden shack was amazing, full of oversized furniture and tons of books. There was one large wooden chair which sat in front of the open fireplace waiting to be sat in. The fire felt warm on the boys' cold faces. Herrif carefully shut the massive doors and then offered everyone a drink of warm herbal senett tea.

The tea was warming and was made of ten thousand different herbs from Fentwell.

Zezma nodded, thanking Herrif, knowing of the tea's warmth and comfort. The boys and Taff nodded as Herrif made his way towards his kitchen. The sleety snow had ceased completely now but the rain and wind howled outside like a banshee. The snow high above on the Brittle Mountains of Smor grew deeper and deeper with every second. No one dared go up these mountains in these conditions, not even the hardiest Tippling would venture further than the wooden bridge across the start of the river of Asbadan.

Herrif returned from the kitchen then sat in the inviting wooden chair by the fireside. They all sipped their tea as the herbs raced around their cold bodies. Hailstones lashed against the roof trying their best to enter the room and dampen the moment. Herrif stroked his long, matted beard and finished his drink first. He placed his mug next to Taff, which was almost the same size as the small terrier.

He then asked Zezma about the Master and what he had done. The Tippling explained about his time on Earth and the glass coffin case. He then told him about the Grotchins.

Herrif sat up in his seat abruptly and looked alert, he had heard of the Grotchins but luckily had not come into contact with them as far as he knew. Zezma continued and asked if the Master had been back to Fentwell. Herrif frowned and thought for a second. He explained that no strangers had been past the gates for at least two years.

Zezma wasn't too sure if the giant was correct. He gazed at the Guardian and asked him again, this time peering deep into his tiny dark brown eyes. The herbal tea was making Zezma stronger, he could feel the magic rushing through his veins like a steam train. He asked Herrif again if anybody had passed the gates.

The Guardian was now in a trance and his eyes rolled backwards and forwards in his colossal head. He mumbled to himself as Zezma moved forward. Herrif slumped in his chair and looked down towards the ground. Zezma repeated the words as the giant lifted his head, his eyes had turned completely white. His muscles stiffened as he rose to his feet. The gang looked on nervously.

"BEGONE FROM HERE" bellowed the Guardian, his eyes still as white as snow.

The fire cracked in the corner as he moved closer towards the large front door. His balance became unstable and Zezma knew evil forces were in control. Herrif tried desperately to fight off the evil and give Zezma his answer but it was useless. He crashed to the floor with a massive thud and the ground shuddered. Daniel raced towards the Guardian and held up his huge head which was the size of a medicine ball. Blood dripped from his brow as Zezma placed a leaf from his bag across the friendly giant's head. The bulk of a giant lay motionless on the cottage floor. The Tippling knew this was bad news, the Master's evil was closer than he thought, he could smell it.

He frowned and gazed at the gentle giant. His senses again smelt the Grotchins, he shivered thinking of the idea of battling them. Herrif blinked and slowly opened his tiny brown eyes. He sat up and then apologised to his new friends. The Guardian stood up and carefully made his way back towards his seat once more. The Tippling opened his cloth bag and removed the tiny Fentwell's book of spells putting it onto the large table in the middle of the room. The book quickly sprung excitedly into its normal size, ready for another journey. Herrif's eyes widened as he caught a glimpse of the mighty book.

"The great lost book of Fentwell" smiled the Guardian "you've found it".

Zezma smiled back. The book sat alone on the table as Zezma reached over and tried to turn its cover. The book sprang into life. Everyone looked on as Zezma leaned down and started to turn one of its mighty pages. The book didn't need any help at all, it knew exactly what the Tippling wanted and started to reveal what Zezma was dreading.

The scene was terrifying. A man wearing a long black cloak at least six-foot-tall with evil piercing eyes stood sideways in front of the Guardian's home. Four muscular creatures sat on oily black snorting horses waiting for the evil man to do his deed. The scene exploded into the room like in the Witch's cottage as the boys, Taff, Herrif, and Zezma looked on terrified.

The Master spoke quietly at first asking the Guardian to let him pass. As usual, Herrif declined and ordered him to leave. Suddenly the blue sky above Herrif's head blackened as the man asked again, this time more sternly.

The tall thin man's voice had deepened, and everything around them had turned cold. The blazing Fentwell sunshine disappeared and hid behind the pitch-black clouds gathering above that seemed to appear from nowhere. The day was quickly cast into night. Herrif stood stunned and motionless, he couldn't reply. The man didn't ask next time, he bellowed, slamming his staff on the Fentwell grassland.

"I COMMAND YOU TO OPEN THESE, GATES NOW"

Herrif gazed on from his chair at the horrific scene played out in front of him. He watched with bulging eyes, he had never seen such a horrible and terrifying sight.

Suddenly, in the scene, Herrif's body arched in agony and thudded to the grassy floor. The evil man walked past with ease and looked down in triumph. One of the horsemen jumped from his black beast and snatched the large gate key from Herrif's leather belt and quickly unlocked the gates bowing to his Master as he passed.

Herrif couldn't move, the evil Master had cast his first spell of the day, many more were to come. A horrible burning sensation entered Herrif's stomach like a bullet from a rifle. This spell was nothing compared to what the Master could really do. This was just the start. The horseman quickly opened the gates and the master stood gazing at the City of Smor once more. The Master sneered then looked towards the large mountain range in front of his eyes. He raised his staff towards the black Fentwell sky and cast another dark and evil spell.

Beware of me and shiver,
My pathway you should never cross,
If you dare, I'll give you agony,
Your life, my gain, your loss.

The Master's spell was now cast, any of his evil followers including the Grotchins could now pass the great gates with ease. Herrif looked on again at the scene watching his body lying crippled on the grassy Fentwell floor. He groaned in agony as the spell engulfed his mass. The magic was strong and held Herrif in agony for hours. When the spell ceased, the mighty Guardian would remember nothing of the Master's passing.

The scene from the great book dulled in the room as the Master slowly walked towards the small City of Smor. The great Brittle Mountains of Smor had shed a tear and cascaded snowy avalanches down the mountains when the Master had raised his bellowing voice. The Tippling families shivered in their small mud hut homes. They knew what was coming and they knew their land and their children would be drained of life once more.

The Master's horsemen followed him closely and the black stallions snorted as sweat and steam dispersed from their black shiny bodies. The evil scene from the great book returned to its pages and left the room feeling cold and damp. Evil had truly stepped into the Guardian's home.

The room lay silent as everyone shivered and then came to their senses. Only the fire spoke as it cracked its red embers. The book slammed shut again with a bang. Zezma looked on at his friends who now knew what the Master was capable of. They all sat quietly as the fire spurted back into life. Herrif raised his head and, embarrassed, apologised for not remembering. The Tippling nodded his head and didn't say a word.

Zezma knew there was more and once again gazed deeply into the Guardian's tiny brown eyes. Herrif sat still as the Tippling entered his mind again.

Zezma saw a vision in his mind, it revealed what he'd been thinking since he'd left the Witches cottage earlier. It was the Grotchins. They had also passed the guardian earlier with total ease, the Master's magic was surely stronger than his.

In the scene, Zezma saw the Grotchins who were disguised as Tipplings. The Grotchins nodded at the giant and sniggered as they passed through the great gates into the City of Smor with ease. The Master's spell had indeed clouded Herrif's thoughts and the three Grotchins moved on towards the Master's lair high up in the mountains above the small city, where Huckle lay with his four soldiers.

Zezma stood up and then stirred the embers in the fireplace. The fire gathered its last bit of life and burst its flames into the room. The Tippling placed a few logs onto the fire as the room slowly warmed up. He sat back down and told everyone to listen carefully.

Zezma sat everyone down and decided this was the right time to explain all he knew about the Master. The horrific stories came out thick and fast. The worst one was about the time when the Master lived on Earth seventy years earlier.

Nearly all the village of Bont and the surrounding villages and towns had fallen into the Master's evil and horrible ways. Murders would happen and nobody would care. People and animals would go missing and still, nobody would care. This was a scary and evil time in the valley.

The Master only left when a local man named

Harry Bell, the eldest of a family of four, gave up his life for the whole valley. The man challenged the Master on one windy, stormy Sunday night in the local church grounds. The Master thought Harry would be a pushover and cast spell after spell against him, but this young man's sheer strength and determination held off the Master for days.

Huckle was exhausted and told his enemy he would leave Earth if he gave him his soul. Harry's cruel death indeed sent the Master back to his moon of Dantra, but Huckle would never forget the look in the man's eyes as he took his last breath.

The stories of the Master had finished as the Tippling rose to his feet and told his friends they could return to Earth if they didn't want to carry on. The boys and Taff stood up not saying a word.

Tim, who hadn't spoken for hours, shivered at the thought of the Master. Zezma didn't mention his vision of the Grotchins in Herrif's eyes, he thought the boys had had enough to deal with for one day.

Herrif lifted his head and grinned at the little terrier. Taff wagged his tail and moved towards the Guardian's door. The Tippling shook Herrif's hand and told him they would meet again one day. Each of the boys shook the giant's hand as they left the warmth of the lovely wooden shack. Herrif knelt and patted the terrier once more, Taff loved the attention and wagged his tail like a helicopter blade. Not many words were said for the next few minutes, but the Tippling knew he had made real friends. Friends that he would die for.

The gang slowly made their way along the meadow as the cold wind and rain chilled their bones. They slowly continued their journey towards the icy cold city of Smor. The Guardian waved them off then bowed his head and returned to his home.

The gang saw the city in the distance, firelight flickered on the seven tall timber lookout spots scattered around its perimeter. The Tipplings in the village were scared, and they hid their children knowing bad times lay ahead.

The Master was upon them.

Beware of the Master.

Chapter 10
The Pathway

After casting one of his easiest spells on the Guardian of the gates the Master turned and smiled to himself and then laughed wickedly. He marched forward towards the City of Smor as his four horsemen walked closely behind him. The Master had many soldiers who guarded him, first were the Hensmen, strong soldiers who guarded the Master with their lives.

Next the scar faced Trivits, who joined Huckle after the great battle for the moon of Dantra. Then there were the Andalights, tall skinny goblin-like creatures who always loved a battle, and finally the mighty evil Grotchins. Grotchins were the most loyal of all, extremely strong and always ready to die for the Master.

The Grotchins had lived on the moon of Dantra for many years before Huckle had arrived. Huckle saved the Grotchins from starvation and they promised to repay him with their lives. Huckle grinned again devilishly, knowing that the Tipplings were in hiding and his delight sent shivers down every living creature in Fentwell.

He told his youngest horseman to stand down

from his horse, which he did immediately bowing his head, just like his elder did earlier. The horsemen always knew they had to respect the Master. The Master held onto the horse's black mane and then flew himself up onto its back just like a gust of cold wind. The horse raised its head as its armoured headgear clattered against its sweaty forehead. The Master clenched his thighs tight and kicked the horse hard in the ribs. The black stallion even with its might and power did as it was told. The horse bolted off like a rocket as the other horses struggled to follow.

The Brittle Mountains of Smor in front of them hid many secrets, the biggest was the Master's lair. Not one Tippling in Fentwell knew where the master's hideout was. Many a story had been told about the lair, but no one had ever seen or knew it where it was. The journey to the lair was treacherous. The mountain pathway in front of Huckle and his horsemen grew narrower and narrower and more dangerous with every step.

After about twenty minutes the Master dismounted his stallion and ordered one of his soldiers to take hold of the black beast while gazing at his surroundings. His black eyes widened with joy and he grinned as he carefully walked further along, nearer and nearer towards his lair. His hands gripped the shale cliff wall, holding it tightly as his long black cloak floated alongside him in the wind like a ghost.

Below him to his left stood a sheer drop of at least three hundred feet. Black stone shaped spikes raised high up into the air from the cold frozen lake of Derelin below, ready to skewer any victim willing to join them. One false step from Huckle along the treacherous pathway and the story of the Tippling

Tales would be over.

The wind howled along through the valley and swirled like a twister. The path with its icy covering made the next two hundred yards barely passable. The horsemen held tightly onto the reins of their horses as the beasts trod carefully foot by foot across the snowy terrain. Suddenly one of the largest black beasts lost its foothold and bolted violently.

The beast charged along the pathway and slid onto its back with a loud crash. The Master's eyes bulged out of his head as he stood close to the edge of the mountain. The beast was sliding right in his direction.

The large black stallion came to a halt ten feet in front of the Master and then quickly tried to struggle to its feet. It stumbled closer towards the pathway's edge. The horse snorted loudly sweat dripping from under its heavy armour. It was too late, the skewers below were about to take their first casualty for many a year.

Huckle gazed on with his bulging black eyes as the horse slid towards the edge of the cliff, then toppled in slow motion off the footpath down into the deep dark hell of Derelin below. The Master snarled at his solider as one of his prize assets fell horribly to its death.

The petrified Grotchin soldier turned his head and looked away, not daring to look into the Master's eyes. The soldier, soaked to the bone and shaking with fear, could feel the Master's anger tangling like barbed wire deep into his brain like a migraine.

The heavens above opened as tears of white snowflakes covered the Master's grimace. The beast had gone, and there was nothing he could do about it.

Huckle removed his eyes from his failure and scrambled his way over the last bit of pathway. He stood motionless waiting for his soldier's and the remaining three black beasts to join him.

The black-armoured soldiers battled against the now blinding snow and slowly made their way across the slippery and dangerous pathway towards their leader. The wind howled down the valley like a screaming witch as the snow fell heavier and heavier. One by one they all gazed at the deep dark cave in the mountainside behind their Master.

Snow now covered most of the entrance to the cave but Huckle was pleased, he knew he would be safe here in his lair, preparing himself to defeat the Tipplings. As the soldiers approached the widening cave entrance the Master greeted them one by one. His black evil eyes stood out against the white soft snow as his black cloak lifted in the wind and flapped down loudly echoing into the cave's depths behind him.

Creatures in the cave all ran deeper into the huge long cavern knowing Huckle and his evil were close. The Master walked over towards the last horseless soldier and patted him hard on his snow-covered back. The soldier bowed his head knowing he had failed by losing the horse earlier. The Grotchin could sense the Master's evil and waited for his punishment. The second pat on his back was harder but the third would be his last. The Grotchin was about to enter his hell.

With a sudden sharp push and a horrible devilish scream from Huckle, the solider was gone. The screaming Grotchin's voice echoed into the valley as he fell into his black hole of death.

Huckle was now very angry and the whole of Fentwell felt it. He turned and faced the valley in front of him, removing his hooded cloak from his head to reveal his devilish evil looks. Snow landed on his long dark hair and slipped off quickly onto the ground below. The Master was furious, and his bellowing voice would be heard for miles below on the stormiest day in over a hundred years.

"FAIL ME" screamed the angered Huckle, holding his staff towards the soldier's black death hole as snow and ice built up in his long grey beard, "and I will bring curses and death upon you all"

The white snow tears in the sky increased in the wind as the remaining Grotchin soldiers held on tightly to their beasts, knowing their lives depended on it. The Master didn't even look at his three remaining soldiers and slowly carried on towards the warmth of his evil dark lair. Huckle was tired and needed rest before he took control of the city below.

A large yew tree covered in snow that had grown on the mountains of Smor for thousands of years stood feet away from the cave's entrance. Snow hung heavily from its branches ready to snap off as Huckle walked into the cave. The mountains above roared with anger and fear, releasing an avalanche of snow cascading down into the valley below. It wouldn't be long, and the Master would be able to regain his strength in the warmth of the cave's dark surroundings.

Finally, battling the wind and snow, the Master walked deep into the entrance of the cave and stood tall gazing at the large wooden doors in front of him. Drops of ice fell off his grey beard and shattered onto the ice cave floor below. The evil Master grinned and edged closer towards the lair's entrance. He stepped forward and shook the snow off his long dark black cloak. He gazed back at his soldiers who were still stood out in the elements, they didn't move a muscle.

He raised his cold evil withered hand and waved at them to follow him in. The three soldiers quickly made their way towards the cave's shelter. Huckle was back and his strength and spells would only get stronger from here. He tapped the heavy oak doors with his staff three times, waited then tapped eight more. The big heavy doors creaked open, welcoming the Master home.

He smirked evilly then walked into the jet-black cave in front of him. Thirteen candles on the cave's walls lit up by magic as he took his first steps into the dark cold cave. He was back but he needed food and rest. Tomorrow he would conquer Fentwell once and for all. The Tipplings would be wiped out for good and the children's memories would be his forever.

The Master edged on deeper into the cave followed closely by his horsemen. The cave grew bigger with every footstep. The Master turned to his soldiers and told them to camp here for the night and not to move or make a sound until morning. The soldiers nodded and tied their horses to some old large tree roots that seemed to move in the darkness. The cave seemed warm compared to the elements outside and the soldiers made themselves comfortable on the cave's floor.

The Master carried on for five more minutes then stopped and tapped his staff on the cave's wall to his left. The wall creaked and groaned as the mountain slowly opened, revealing a tall thin crack. The crack widened revealing another large ancient door. This door was covered with carvings of strange creatures. Some had two heads others with unimaginable horror in their eyes all fighting to leave the doorway and attack its intruders. Carved in the middle of the door was the name of the Master's home.

Raven Cliff Castle

Raven Cliff Castle had been built on the moon of Dantra thousands of years earlier by the mighty goblin tribe the Jenulitts. Behind the doorway lay the Master's lair. Huckle was pleased and placed his cold grey hand onto the cold steel snake-shaped handle. He pushed down on the handle and the door creaked loudly echoing into the tunnels and caves in the mountain. He took his first step into his lair as candles once again lit by magic. Huckle was back and his evil was now truly inside the mountain.

Back outside the City of Smor, the Grotchins from Bont finally reached the end of the meadow and noticed Herrif the giant sitting by the large oak gates eating a huge giant mole sandwich. Whizzer drooled at the thought and gazed on as saliva dripped from his chapped lips. Alfren stood and gazed at the huge man and thought of a plan.

Suddenly the giant lifted his nose and smelt trouble, he stood tall and ordered them to show themselves. Alfren stepped forward and ordered the guardian Herrif to open the gates. His two companions stood tall next to him. The guardian frowned then held up his staff and tried desperately to disagree but suddenly the Master's forces entered his head like a bullet. Alfren wiped his sweaty brow and moved on as Herrif fell to his knees with a heavy thud. Herrif was under the Master's spell. A spell of pain and despair.

The eldest Grotchin sensed the Master's powers as he and his two companions walked past with ease. Herrif lay crippled in agony on the floor as his stomach swirled like the storm down the valley. The wind raced through Alfren's greasy hair as he walked along the pathway towards the mighty Brittle Mountains of Smor that lay in front of him. The city was engulfed either side by huge cliffs and this route through the city was the only way passable to the great mountains.

The two moons above sneaked out of the stormy dark clouds and shone brightly, lighting up the pathway towards the mountains and the Master's lair. Alfren looked high into the mountains and shivered. This shivering was not with cold, this shivering was of fear, total fear. He knew the Master would not be happy and hoped he would be spared when they met.

The three Grotchins moved on with their task. The three of them knew that when they met the Master something terrible was going to happen to at least one of them. They could be replaced easily. They moved on and headed up the mountainside. The snow was now falling heavily, and the pathway was nearly unpassable. The lair was getting closer but so also was the Master. They walked in silence awaiting their fate. The snow was now in blizzard conditions and the pathway soon became unrecognizable. The three figures struggled on as the snow covered their bodies like a white bed sheet.

The wind blew violently into their faces as tears fell from their eyes freezing before they hit the ground. Whizzer crouched behind Alfren and whimpered with every footstep. Alfren held his head low and moved on closer towards the lair. The twinkle of the fires below in the city faded with every footstep. The avalanche earlier had blocked the pathway and the Grotchins struggled to keep their footing. They scrambled through the snowdrifts desperately trying to find the pathway again.

Whizzer slipped as he leapt down from the snowdrift sliding on his back heading to certain death in the darkness below. Alfren grabbed him by his matted hair at the last minute and dragged him back onto the path. Suddenly from nowhere, the wind dropped, and the snow stopped like magic. The skies that were once black and filled with snow were now blue and clear. Was this a good thing or a bad thing?

The black daggered skewers below showed themselves as the Grotchins held tightly onto the cliff's edge. Suddenly two hundred yards in front of the Grotchins stood the snow-covered yew tree with its heavy-laden arms. Without this bit of Huckle magic, the Grotchins would have never found the entrance of the cave.

Alfren could feel the presence of his Master and thought about his fate once more. Slowly they moved along and passed the old yew tree towards the doorway of the cave. As they stood at the cave's entrance the storm took hold once more, hiding the entrance behind them. Frozen snow hung onto their face like leeches. The Master's three Grotchin soldiers had made it. They entered the cave and shook the snow from their frozen bodies. A feeling of terror entered the three brothers like a tornado. Their fate for letting the Tippling escape was close.

A deafening scream of rage from the master raced through the tunnels in the dark cave in front of them. Huckle sat in his lair awaiting his failures. The Grotchins soon stood next to their fellow soldiers shivering in the cave and didn't say a word to each other just as the Master had ordered. Alfren took a step forward when suddenly he heard a voice in his head ordering him and him only further into the lair. The eldest Grotchin turned to his brothers and told them to stay where they were.

Alfren walked forward and soon became aware that he was very close to his punishment. The Master sat by his old Wallem Wood table ready for his servant to appear. He reached over and lay two more logs on his cosy fire in the corner of the room. Smoke filled the room as a gust outside whistled down the lair's stone chimney. The room flickered with an amber glow as books of spells and potions stood tall in their bookcase behind the Master's shoulder.

On the large table in front of the Master stood at least ten small bottles, all full of different coloured liquids. Some were harmless and only used for aches and pains, but the small black jars with cork lids held potions that nobody knew of, not even Huckle himself.

Huckle knew the Grotchin was standing outside the door and made him wait as he ate a meal of live bats and worms which moved in his mouth with every spoonful. Huckle licked his lips and then told the Grotchin to enter his room. Alfren stepped through the crack in the mountainside and then through the oak door. Creatures on the doorway seemed to come to life as he passed, snapping and hissing at him with every footstep. Alfren entered his nightmare as the creatures returned to their solid-state.

He held his head low as the Master's eyes peered deep into his soul.

"Where is my prize?" Huckle spoke with what seemed a calm and gentle voice. Alfren knew the prize was Zezma and couldn't say a word. The Master stood up pushing his chair hard against the solid Wallem wooden table.

"WELL" bellowed Huckle with his eyes bulging with anger.

The room filled with smoke again as the wind outside screamed to help the Grotchin, but no wind or spell would save Alfren from this punishment. Huckle stepped forward holding a large black-handled knife in his right hand that he had plucked from the table drawer. Alfren took a step back. The Master told his solider to stand still and place his hand down flat on the table. The Grotchin nervously placed his hand on the table and awaited his fate. With a sudden blow of the razor-sharp knife, the Grotchin's little finger on his left hand fell onto the floor like a large dead slug.

Alfren pulled his hand back in agony but the Master told him to replace it on the table. Alfren showed no fear as any loyal solider would and did as he was told. Blood dripped from the table and sank deep into the dust on the floor of the lair. The Grotchin again showed no fear as the Master raised his knife once more. The knife glistened in the firelight lit room but this time it sliced off part of the Grotchin's left ear. Alfren jumped back and froze as

blood dripped onto his face
"YOU WILL NEVER FAIL ME AGAIN
GROTCHIN DO YOU HEAR?"
said the Master holding part of Alfren's ear in his
hand then carefully placing it into a jar on his table,
screwing the lid down tightly.

"NOW GO" spoke Huckle angrily "next time
you fail me I will take you and one of your brothers
and you will both die a slow and horrid death."

Alfren held his bloodied hand against his ear and
returned through the crack in the wall and back
towards the others. His brothers looked on as Alfren
patched himself up with a leaf from his cloth bag.

Alfren knew tomorrow the Tipplings would be
slain for good. All the Tipplings would be killed once
and for all and the land of Fentwell would belong to
the Master.

Huckle sat by his table gazing at the cave walls in
front of him. His thoughts spun in his head like a
washing machine, looking for the spell that would
help him defeat all the Tipplings. He grinned as the
washing machine slowed down in his head. He then
started to make potions and spells, flicking through
the large book of spells in front of him. "Death to all
my enemies" read one spell, as he looked on at his
father's horrible book of death.

The smoke around the lair darted in and out of
every crack and crevice as each page delivered
unimaginable spells. As he turned the pages, he found
an old spell and grinned again, knowing no one
except his father knew of this spell. The Grotchin's
ear would make it perfect and even stronger.

Huckle slammed his book shut and dust rose off
the table and into the fire lit room. Creatures in jars

on the shelves above his head moved eerily in the light, trying to escape their watery coffins. Huckle floated across the room like a ghost and slid into his wooden bed in the corner of the cave. He slowly lay down, closing his large black eyes and entered a dream of war and victory. In a few hours the battle against the Tipplings would commence and the beautiful land of Fentwell would be gone forever.

Chapter 11
The Hidden Tunnel

Earlier, in the city of Smor, the snowstorm tore through the tiny streets covering absolutely everything. The streets in front of Zezma and his friends were all deserted and deathly quiet. All the Tipplings lay silent in their buried hideaways like meercats.

The snowflakes danced around in the fire lit street like fairies as the snowstorm fell silently. All lay quiet in Smor even the bats and owls were hiding tonight.

Zezma and his friends edged closer towards the Tippling's home when suddenly, ten yards ahead, a large weird-looking creature appeared from behind one of the small mud houses. Its back was enormous and armour-plated like a dinosaur's, but its head was pointed like an alligator.

Zezma quietly told the gang to stop and not to move a muscle. The creature in their sights was a rare night stalking Hugget. A very hungry night stalking Hugget. The creature hissed and smelt the air with its snake-like tongue looking for its next meal. A Tippling alone would make a very nice meal indeed. The beast sniffed some small waste bins with its large snout and rummaged through a large pile of rubbish outside one of the mud huts. Fifty stone of pure muscle walked the streets of Fentwell without a care in the world.

This was one of Huckle's creatures from his homeland, the Moon of Dantra. The Tippling knew things had turned bad; he hadn't seen a Hugget for years. The creature gazed into the gang's direction and sniffed the air once more. Snow covered its back like cotton wool.

The beast moved forward slowly as the gang edged quietly behind one of the mud huts for cover. The beast sniffed the air again then stood up on all fours and let out an ear-thundering roar. The snow on the mountains above shuddered and cascaded down into the small valley. The hungry beast looked again in the direction of the gang as Zezma peered around from the hut. The beast edged closer smelling its prey with every footstep.

Suddenly from nowhere appearing like magic a huge pure white snow snake lifted itself from its hideout in the ground. The snake was at least thirty-foot-long, and its mouth was large enough to swallow a small car.

The Hugget stepped back in surprise and the snake moved forward towards the snarling cowering beast. The pure white snow snake slid itself along the snow-covered ground with ease. The snake was hungry, red saliva dripped from the side of its mouth like tomato ketchup.

Zezma looked on in amazement. He had never seen a snow snake before in his life. He had heard of all the stories but now he was seeing one for real. The snake hissed and moved forward towards its meal. Zezma gazed on as the snake launched itself towards the Hugget. The battle had begun. The hissing and the snorting was deafening. The first bite was on the Hugget's back. The beast screamed in agony as it tried to defend itself. The snake's three vampire-like teeth sunk deep into the Hugget's back, as it hung on tightly and slowly started wrapping its massive body around the creature.

The Hugget tried desperately to release itself but it had no chance. The snake's body was now gripping tightly as the air from the Hugget's throat slowly faded into the winter's night. The Hugget gave one last roar as the snake bit heavily down on the beast's neck. Blood shot across the white snow like a graffiti artist's masterpiece.

Daniel gazed from behind Zezma's head and couldn't believe what he had just seen. The snake's black eyes rolled in its head as it started to devour the beast in what seemed like one big gulp. The Hugget was gone, but the dangerous snow snake was well and truly alive gulping down its meal as if it was going to be its last.

The Hugget's body inside the snake moved down into its stomach like something on a walking elevator. The black-eyed snow snake slivered back towards its hole deep under one of the city's small mud huts. Its stomach churned and gurgled loudly as the acids did their job. Zezma shook his head in disbelief.

Suddenly in front of the gang, next to the mud hut where the beasts had been fighting, appeared what looked like a doorway into the ground. The mighty battle of the beasts had moved tons of snow and soil revealing the double doorway into the unknown.

Zezma gasped and stood motionless. He had

heard of this doorway many times. Many stories about the doorway were told around campfires telling tales of hideouts and caves that led high up into the mountains. Many elder Tipplings would change the subject if asked about the caves, knowing about the Master and the creatures that lay inside. The last Tippling to enter the caves had disappeared and was never seen or heard of again, so the stories said.

Zezma looked on and moved closer towards the doorway. The Tippling knew this must be the shortcut to the mountains but also knew about its dangers. He looked down at the doorway beneath his feet then reached for its cold steel handle. The snow fell heavier as the double oak doorway opened with ease as if wanting its intruders to enter. The snow seemed to stop suddenly and keep away from the entrance and danced off and fell elsewhere. The Tippling looked down deep into the hole in front of him. Thirty steps covered in slime led down into complete darkness. Stories of all the horrors raced into the Tippling's head.

"Whatever you do" whispered Zezma turning round to explain to the gang "Do not touch the poison ivy hanging from the hole's entrance, it's highly poisonous just like acid."

The hole was pitch black and the ivy swung in the wind, dripping its goo onto the walls of the entrance. Zezma lit his Firesinth torch as a million leeches looked at him hungrily. The gang slowly followed the Tippling down the steep steps making sure not to touch anything. Finally, they reached the floor of the cave which had a small stream running through it.

Zezma walked along the cave's wet floor as it narrowed, the group moved forward deep into the

belly of the mountain. As they walked a little further
the Firesinth torch lit up the pathway and the cave
tunnel suddenly split into three. One large cave led to
the mountains, the other back to the river of
Asbadan, and the last one led deep into the heart of
the mountain's with miles and miles of caves with
unknown beasts and spirits.

Zezma stopped and gazed at the caves in front of
him. He had no idea which one to take as no one had
ever been in the cave this far before. Suddenly he
froze and felt a cold presence standing right behind
him. The Master was there, not in body but in spirit.

He shivered again as the Firesinth torch flickered
and shivered with him. Taff growled knowing evil was
close then sniffed the cave floors. The boys looked on
not knowing which cave tunnel to take. Zezma knew
the wrong turn could mean death for them all.

He held his head up high towards the cave ceiling
not knowing what to do when suddenly a vision lit up
on the ceiling above them. It was Huckle. Zezma
watched the vision on the ceiling as his magic grew
stronger. He saw that Huckle had entered his lair and
was resting ready to defeat the Tipplings once and for
all.

The Master was indeed sleeping but he could feel
the presence of the Tippling in his dream and lashed
out at Zezma with his staff. The vision was gone as
quickly as it had appeared.

Zezma had to decide quickly which tunnel to take,
as the time for his beautiful land was running out.
The gang gazed on at the three entrances in front of
them when suddenly Tim noticed something move in
one of the tunnel's entrances. The object quickly
scurried behind one of the large rocks by the entrance

and hissed like a snake.

Zezma held out his staff in front of him and instructed the creature to reveal itself. The creature snarled and slid into the darkest corner it could to hide itself.

Daniel walked forward and asked Zezma what it was. Zezma shook his head and held the torch closer towards the creature which ran across the cave and hid again. Daniel jumped as the creature nearly knocked him over.

Tim darted behind Daniel as Taff growled loudly in the creature's direction. Zezma moved closer and once again told the creature to reveal itself or he would put a Tippling curse on it that would make its life unbearable.

The creature raised its pointed ears and looked up towards the ceiling sniffing the air with his pointed nose. The creature was cautious, it hadn't seen anybody for at least sixty years. Zezma moved the Firesinth closer towards the creature as it hid its appearance again.

Zezma looked in amazement as the creature hunched itself in a defensive position and looked directly into the Tippling's direction still sniffing and smelling the air. Zezma realised the creature in front of him was a Tippling itself, but not one that he had ever seen before. The creature was nearly as white as the snow outside and its eyes had turned completely white with piercing black pupils. Zezma realised the creature was completely blind.

The creature was indeed a Tippling, that exact Tippling that went missing nearly sixty years ago in the hidden tunnels, and it was still alive.

Zezma gasped then explained who he and his

friends were and that they were looking for the
Master to defeat him once and for all. The lost
Tippling shivered and slid back behind the rock. His
fear was felt throughout the gang.

Daniel reached out his hand and asked the lost
Tippling to join them on their journey. The snow-
white Tippling hid and replied with a definite no. He
slowly slid back up moving his head from side to side
and told them his name was Pinnet and that the
Master knew of him. Pinnet would never dare to do
or say anything against the Master.

Zezma asked him if he had ever met him down
here in the tunnels. The lost Tippling replied the
Master only visited the tunnels when he knew he was
in great danger. "He doesn't like the tunnels because
of the lack of air and doesn't know where they all
lead". He said. Pinnet walked forward and held out
his hand towards his fellow Tippling.

"Take my hand young Tippling and I will show
you where I first met the Master and show you what
he did to our people."

Zezma stepped forward and held out his long,
fingered hand. Pinnet grasped it as if he was falling
off a cliff's edge.

"Be prepared my friend, for scenes that your
mind will never forget" said Pinnet, grasping Zezma's
with all his might.

Suddenly a flash of light lit up Zezma's mind like
a laser show. Appearing through a grey mist stood
Huckle, all in black, standing tall in front of all his
soldiers glaring down at all the Tipplings.

"This was a long time ago" explained Pinnet.
The Tipplings in the scene all scattered before his
eyes like a plague of rats. Huckle grinned and

commanded his army to attack. Zezma looked on as Huckle's soldiers in his vision ravished the land of Fentwell.

"Huckle took many memories that day" explained Pinnet "but some of us were lucky, the elders took us to shelter in the hidden tunnels."

Zezma had heard of this story and just looked on amazed by the Master's powers. Pinnet released his grip on Zezma's hand and the vision was gone. The Tippling explained that they all hid down in the tunnels until the Master thought all the Tipplings were dead, but some of them survived, and some are still alive to tell the tale.

Zezma stood motionless looking at the white elder in front of him knowing his enemy was indeed truly evil. Daniel stepped forward and asked Pinnet which tunnel do you think we should take.

Pinnet replied strongly "none of them, leave now and you might be saved."

That wasn't an option. Zezma knew he would have to save the Tipplings because this time Huckle would not stop for anything. He knew Huckle would make sure that all the Tipplings would be slaughtered, every single one of them and no one was going to defeat him.

Zezma stepped up to the first tunnel and asked Pinnet if this was the tunnel that he had been locked in all those years ago. The white Tippling knew Zezma wanted to complete his journey and nodded in agreement then stood up and explained what would happen to him if he told them which tunnel to take.

The story he revealed was a story of horrid death and slow pain, but the white Tippling was tired of his hell below ground.

"The first tunnel on the left", he said, "is full of animals and creatures that no had ever seen or heard of. Horrid and evil things that are always hungry and will eat anything in their pathway. The middle tunnel is the tunnel of a million tunnels, once in never to be released. The third tunnel is the one you will need but by telling you this I know the Master will be angry and my fate in this world will be set. I have heard his evil voice in the tunnels many times through the walls, but this tunnel will lead you to the Master. Huckle doesn't know of these tunnels and if you are going to survive, he must never know."

Zezma reached out and tapped his fellow frail Tippling on the shoulder and asked him to join them. Pinnet refused and explained his death of pain had already started the moment he revealed his secret. He could feel the evil racing through his bloodstream as they spoke. The pure white tippling knelt as the pain increased in his ageing bones.

Huckle's evil spell took control as the Tippling held back the pain and forced a smile from his shivering body. The gang looked on into the darkest hole in the mountain and thanked the Tippling for his help.

"Before you go my friends" said, Pinnet, gripping onto a greasy rock for support "Please beware of the green bats, roof leeches and especially the dark bloodsucking redrings."

The gang moved on anxiously then nodded, knowing nothing of the creatures that lay ahead of them. They moved on into the tunnel as Daniel whispered into Tim's ear.

"Bloodsucking redrings?"

Tim just shook his head and carried on walking

deeper and deeper into the belly of the mountain. Pinnet writhed in agony as the Master's spell took control. He sensed the gang moving down the tunnel as the Firesinth torch got smaller and smaller with every footstep. Water dripped from the ceiling of the cave dropping heavily onto the floor echoing into the distance like a large clock. Suddenly the light of the fire torch had gone. The gang were indeed now deep into the belly of the mountain and Huckle was waiting.

Pinnet collapsed into a heap on the floor as his life drifted away. The spell from the evil Master released him from his hell in the dark secret tunnels of Smor.

Chapter 12
The Master's Lair

Zezma led the way down the deep dark tunnel but then stopped suddenly as he felt a presence directly in front of them. The tunnel was so dark you couldn't see further than the end of your arm. Everyone stopped and listened as Taff sniffed the air loudly.

Zezma shivered as the cave suddenly started to get colder and colder. The Firesinth torch spluttered and struggled to stay alight and then suddenly the gang were in complete darkness. Their eyes struggled to adjust to the blackness as Zezma tried desperately to relight the fire torch. The tunnel was silent, freezing cold and pitch black. The gang stood shivering not knowing what lay ahead.

Suddenly a deafening high-pitched screeching filled the tunnel. The gang all covered their ears in agony as the noise grew louder. Suddenly the screaming stopped then two bright red eyes about the size of pound coins appeared on the wall in front of Zezma and the gang.

Taff snarled as the eyes moved over the tunnel's

walls with ease. Suddenly two more appeared followed by what seemed like a thousand staring red eyes. The ceiling, the ground and all the floor were now covered in blood-red pound coins, but these red coins were hungry, and today's dinner looked tasty. The objects moved quickly and surrounded the gang like an army of red ants, but these weren't red ants at all.

Zezma struggled again in the cold, trying to light the fire torch as the screeching got louder but then suddenly stopped as quickly as it started. The red eyes all scurried off the walls, floor, and ceiling and seemed to form a red barrier behind the gang. Now thousands of eyes gazed in the pitch-black cold tunnel waiting for something to happen. The blood-red eyes knew what was coming and licked their fangs with hungry excitement.

Zezma and his friends had no idea what lay in front of them. The tunnel was silent again, only the growling of Taff could be heard echoing down the dark tunnels. The gang knew they couldn't go back but daren't think what was in front of them.

Something moved in the pitch-black tunnel, scratching the walls with its razor-sharp claws. The scratching on the walls grew louder as Taff barked sharply, the noise bouncing off the walls and quickly escaping to the safety of the tunnels behind the thousand red eyes.

Foul-smelling odour filled their nostrils like a pit of a thousand dead animals. The scratching noise scraped along the ceiling walls and the floor like sharp nails against a sheet of metal. Whatever was in front of them was huge and filled the tunnel. No way forward and no way back.

The blood-red eyes behind the gang shone brightly and waited patiently for the scene in front of them to explode. Hunger filled their rumbling bellies. Their last meal was over two months ago, and they were all ready for their next one.

Zezma desperately tried to light his Firesinth torch again and in doing so caught a glimpse of what lay in front of him. He froze to the spot and shivered. The creature with its plate-sized red eyes and black dripping fangs was about to taste its first-ever Tippling. Zezma didn't know what to do to help his friends and felt the fear shiver down his spine like an icy waterfall.

The creature moved closer as did its offspring. The tunnel was now freezing. Redring Spider's ideal conditions for eating, the colder the better. Closer and closer the mother and her offspring moved towards their prey. Zezma, Daniel, Tim and Taff couldn't do anything. Was this it? The end of their adventures, of their lives?

Something was about to happen that the Tippling had known would happen the first time he met the Earth boy. Daniel shivered with fear, placing his hands deep in his pocket desperately trying to keep warm. Suddenly he felt the Wallem Witch's dust tingle in his fingernails. Was this the answer?

The spider screeched its loudest screech which echoed around the mountain and reached Pinnet's dying ears. Pinnet bowed his head and knew they had met the Redrings. He knew a horrible death awaited them.

Daniel felt the tingling again then grabbed hold of the dust particles in his pocket and threw them blindly into the direction of the screeching beast. The tunnel exploded into the brightest light it had ever seen, just like the flash of a nuclear explosion. The boys and Zezma and Taff closed their eyes and covered their faces. The Redrings screamed in agony, mother and offspring ran off in all directions in agonizing pain. Redrings have no eyelids and the explosion of the Wallem Witch dust light blinded them as they all raced back to the safety of their nest deep in the darkest cave of the Tunnels of Smor.

Zezma took his hands from his eyes and couldn't believe what had just happened. The light of the flash started easing as the Redrings all disappeared. The odour was still foul, but they were alive. Zezma smiled at the boys and realised that Daniel had more strengths than he had ever imagined.

The gang moved forward and Zezma knew the lair was close. He tried again to light his Firesinth torch and this time it lit. The pathway in front of them was covered in Redrings slime. Thick goo dripped off the walls onto the tunnel's floors. The tunnels started getting narrower and narrower with every footstep.

Acid leeches fell from the ceiling, burning cigarette sized holes into the Tippling's back. Daniel flicked each one off with his fingertips as his friend moved closer and closer towards the Master's lair. Green bats swooped down with needle-pointed fangs trying desperately to grasp a slice of blood. The gang fended them off and moved forward. The tunnel grew smaller and smaller and Zezma had to bow his head to get through.

Suddenly the tunnel in front of them ended abruptly. Wet black rock stood directly in front of the gang's eyes. Zezma looked puzzled and gazed at the cold dark wall in front of him.

"This can't be it" said Zezma, gazing at the wall. "Is this a trick of the Master?"

Zezma raised his head and closed his eyes then looked deep into his mind for some kind of answer. Every time he closed his eyes the Master was always there, smiling devilishly. The solid rock formation in front of them seemed to move for a second. Daniel looked again but the rock stood still. Maybe it was a trick of the Firesinth torch.

Zezma locked in his visions suddenly smiled as he realized what was in front of him. He shook the vision from his mind and walked straight up to the rock face putting his right hand straight through the wall of the cave like a magician. He turned to his friends, then smiled in the Firesinth torchlight and stepped forward, walking straight through the wall.

Zezma disappeared, leaving the tunnel in total darkness. Daniel and Tim grabbed hold of each other as Taff shivered by their feet. Two seconds seemed like two hours, but the Tippling was back and told his friends to follow him through the wall. Daniel, Tim and Taff followed Zezma and moved ever closer towards the Master. The lair was close. Huckle's magic was strong, Zezma could feel it in his bones.

When they appeared on the opposite side of the wall, the tunnel had turned into a small hole just big enough to crawl through. Zezma went first holding the fire torch in front of him followed closely by Daniel then Tim and Taff. The tunnel wasn't very long and Zezma crawled out the hole and discovered he was standing on a ledge high above the rock face where the Grotchins had rested earlier.

Unknown to Zezma, the Grotchins and the

Master had gone. Huckle had awoken from his dreams and decided this was the time. This was the time he was going to conquer the land of Fentwell and make it the land on which he was going to survive and live forever.

The two Fentwell moons shone in the sky as he and his soldiers moved out of the cave and headed into the elements. The moons had risen, but the dark snow clouds and the bitterly cold wind soon asserted their authority and covered the sky once more.

Zezma scrambled down the crumbling rock face with his friends as the smell of the Grotchins filled the air. The next tunnel in front of them was indeed the passage to the lair. They edged forward with caution. Taff went in front and soon came upon the crack in the mountainside. Zezma knew this was it and squeezed himself through the crack to face his evil enemy.

In front of him stood the doorway. Huckle entered his mind and he didn't know what to expect when he opened the large oak carved door to face his worst nightmare.

He placed his hand on the door handle. A burning sensation like Daniel's earlier at the mansion entered his hand but he battled through the pain. The doorway creaked open and Daniel held his nose as the foul-smelling Grotchin's odour again raced into his nostrils.

The whole lair was covered in a fine golden coloured dust, which flickered in the Firesinth light. In the corner was an old fireplace with cobwebs hanging down from its mantelpiece. Large hairy spiders ran everywhere to escape the light. There were old leather-bound books covered in dust lying everywhere. Zezma stepped forward and immediately knew Huckle had gone. He felt immense relief but also dread because he knew where he was heading.

On a table in the middle of the room was the book of death and a large glass jar like a goldfish bowl with something moving inside. The goldfish bowl had a lid on, closed tightly. Inside it was the darkest spellbinding creature known to the dark side.

"What is it?" questioned Daniel looking over towards Zezma. The Tippling had no idea, he had never seen anything like it before.

"That's not a creature from Fentwell" explained Zezma looking at the five-headed snake like creature.

The creature hissed and snarled as the gang moved closer to look. It spat its black venom at them which slowly slid down the inside of the glass goldfish bowl. One drop of the creature's venom was enough to kill an entire army. Zezma slowly made his way towards the table, telling everyone not to touch anything.

The creature, which was now changing colours like a chameleon as it blended into its surroundings in the goldfish bowl making itself invisible. This was Huckle's prize for winning a magician's contest that had been held in the land of Gan over a hundred years ago. Its powers were totally unknown, but all dark magicians in the universe had heard of this creature, **The Ransit**. Huckle knew of its powers and was going to unlock them but Fentwell and all the Tippling deaths came first.

Zezma carefully opened the lid. The creature inside with five heads screamed and hissed as it opened, then the whole room filled with a terrible odour. Zezma quickly screwed back down the lid before the creature could make its exit. Tim held Zezma's fire torch right in front of the jar trying to get a better view. To his horror, the creature leapt forward snarling at the bright light. Tim stumbled back, then quickly handed the torch back to the Tippling.

"The Master's powers are stronger than I ever imagined" whispered Zezma.

"Where do you think he is?" asked Daniel still gazing at the horrible creature slithering around in the jar trying desperately to attack the Earth boy.

Zezma turned then looked at Daniel for a second. His eyes turned white like Pinnet's as he gazed into the depths of the deep dark lair. The Tippling had gone into trace once again. In his trance, he was following the Master and his soldiers down the snowy pathway towards the city of Fentwell.

"No" screamed the Tippling angrily putting his hand to his head. He knew where Huckle was, and he knew he had to hurry.

Huckle was now only five hundred yards from the city and licked his lips of the thought of all the Tippling children's memories. He knew when he had taken all the memories, he would look young and feel strong again. He held many in his mind from previous visits but this time he would take them all and eat the Tippling's leader's heart, making sure every one of them would die.

Zezma looked around and shook his head then started putting things in his cloth bag as quickly as he could. The jar with the creature in went into the bag first followed by two more small jars with red liquid in swirling like tornados.

Daniel picked up things and again put them in his

pocket like the Wallem Witch dust.

Zezma reached up to the mantelpiece as a picture of Huckle's father glared down at him in the dusty Firesinth light. Zezma didn't even look as he grabbed a book off the mantelpiece and placed in his bag. The book refused at first and struggled but Zezma forced it in, knowing a bit of the Master's evil would always help him to conquer Huckle. The Tippling turned and told his followers to move quickly. The gang moved out of the lair as the room quickly darkened leaving a small glow where the fire had been. Huckle's father glared down again out of the dusty oil painting on the wall as his enemies left the lair, his eyes bulging with evil just like his son's.

The gang climbed back up the crumbling rock face and soon found themselves in the tunnels on their way back towards the city.

The battle of good and evil was about to begin.

Chapter 13
Helta

Huckle shook the snow off his long black cloak as he slowly entered the small snow-covered City of Smor. The wind blew through his hair as he moved closer towards the centre of the city. Every footstep he took left a black footprint behind him.

Alfren, his brothers and the other Grotchins followed closely on their horses. The armour on the black stallions clanked loudly as the wind ceased and the city lay deathly quiet. Snow fell quietly on the already thickly covered paths.

Huckle walked through the city looking for one child, and one Tippling child only. He knew the capture of this particular Tippling would cripple Zezma to his core and knew he could easily win the battle with this prize.

Out of the thirty-eight children that had lived in Smor all those years ago, Huckle had taken eleven. These children were still alive but lived a life of no smiles, no laughter and no fun. Huckle had taken all that from them. He walked slowly, passing ten Tippling houses on his left then stopped and looked directly in front of him. This was Zezma's old house.

The clouds parted as the two moons shone brightly onto the Tippling's small house like a spotlight revealing the way. Huckle walked forward opened the gate and stepped onto the snow-covered garden path. Alfren followed with his brothers as the remaining Grotchins waited outside the garden. The horses snorted as moisture left their nostrils like steam from a steam train.

The Tipplings inside knew danger was near and shivered in their underground hideout.

Huckle walked over towards the doorway and tapped his staff three times against the wooden door. The snow continued to fall as the evil Master prepared for his first Tippling feast of the night. The Tipplings hid deep under their houses in cave-like dwellings, dreading the evil that was about to enter their lives.

Zezma's mother and father huddled together in the corner of their hideout with their daughter, Helta.

Huckle ordered Alfren to burst down the door which he did with one blow of his mighty arm.

"Reveal yourselves now or die a crippling death of pain and horror" said Alfren.

The silence was deafening, the snow outside was louder than the reply.

Alfren screamed again, but still nothing. Huckle glanced around the room and stood glaring at the floorboards below him. He grinned as saliva from his hungry lips dropped onto the wooden floor boards then pointed his finger towards the floor. The eldest Grotchin threw the table across the room and ripped the cloth rug from the wooden flooring. A trap door appeared in front of them as the Tipplings below shivered knowing evil had entered their house.

Alfren ripped open the trapdoor as Huckle ordered the Tipplings up from their hideout, threating to kill them all. The Tippling family, led by Zezma's father Zenton, moved towards the wooden ladder which led to the hell above.

Zenton held Helta close then secretly hid her in a secret passage next to the wooden ladder. He and his beloved wife climbed the ladder and entered the room they once thought safe. Huckle looked on waiting for the child to appear but angrily growled when she didn't.

"HELTA" growled Huckle, with anger and gripping tightly to his staff in his right hand "Bring her to me now".

Zenton told him Helta had left the City of Smor last year and she had moved to a small village called Tannets at the end of the great wood. Huckle slashed Zenton across his face with his wand sending him flying into the corner of the room.

Zenton's wife Heltaenna stepped forward as Huckle stood above her like a vampire ready to taste her blood.

"BRING HER TO ME NOW OR YOU, YOUR FAMILY AND ALL THE TIPPLINGS WILL DIE"

Heltaenna ran over towards her husband who stood up, just as Helta stepped off the last rung of the ladder and entered the room. The Master grinned and told her to sit on the chair directly in front of him. Zenton rushed forward, trying to stop her as Alfren locked him in his slimy grey arms.

Helta sat on the cold wooden chair shivering with fear as Whizzer stood next to her grinning waiting for her fate.

"Look at me Helta" grinned Huckle "join me".

Helta looked away, gazing at her crying mother but soon enough Huckle gazed into her eyes and her memories were gone. Her childhood memories were now the Master's and he laughed deviously as the strength of the spell rushed through his veins.

Alfren let go of his grip on Zenton as Heltaenna cried in the corner. Helta was gone, only her shell remained. Huckle felt strong and laughed as he turned and left the cold cottage.

"I need more" he roared "bring me more".

Zezma came to a shuddering halt when he heard the Master screaming his sister's name and knew his family was in great danger. He rushed through the caves and tunnels desperately trying to find his way out. Each tunnel led to another then another. It was useless they were stuck. Fourteen tunnels appeared around the next corner leading to fourteen more than another fourteen more. The gang stopped, panting heavily after all their running.

"Wait" said Daniel "We must wait and listen"

Zezma looked at Daniel frowning, knowing his sister and family were in terrible danger.

"Listen" said the Earth boy again.

Daniel held his hand to his ear and told everyone to be quiet. Tunnel one nothing, tunnel two three and up to tunnel nine, nothing. But tunnel ten had a distant trickling noise coming from its depths. Zezma stepped into the tunnel and heard the trickling water.

"When we entered the tunnels there was a stream" explained Daniel.

Zezma looked at Daniel, grinned then raced into the tenth dark tunnel. The tunnel was narrow at first but then opened widely, it was indeed the way out.

Back in Smor, Huckle walked away from Zezma's parents house knowing he had the most important thing in his grasp, Helta's memories, and that Zezma would do or give anything to get them back. The Master chuckled as he walked through the snow-covered paths with his soldiers, towards his next victims.

Suddenly, around the next corner, he saw thirty strong Tippling men, all armed with sticks and Tippling spells. The Master laughed as Alfren stepped forward to face the pathetic enemy in his path.

The first Tippling stepped forward sending a spell that hit Alfren hard against his chest throwing him to the hard, frozen ground. Alfren, shocked, stood up and looked at the Master. Never before had any Tipplings spells worked so well.

Huckle snarled and from his black cloak pocket threw a handful of Dantra dust across the snowy battleground. At once a thousand small rat-like creatures all with vampire bat teeth, ran towards their prey. The Tippling's all stepped back as the rats raced towards them. The eldest Tippling, named Strontar, stepped forward and cast a Tippling spell, just as the first of the rats were about to pounce. The rats all turned into black dust and fell onto the white ground like soot.

Huckle looked on amazed. Never had Tipplings fought so hard before. Strontar stepped forward again with his army close behind and told Huckle and his soldiers to leave. If they didn't, he would turn them into pillars of salt where they stood. Huckle looked at the strong muscular Tippling in front of him and knew he was the leader. It was this Tippling's heart he would have to eat if the battle for Fentwell was to be won.

Huckle opened his cloak and removed the jar that he had picked up earlier in the lair. The Grotchin's ear lay in the jar still covered in blood. The Grotchins stepped back as he placed the red half ear on the white snowy ground, its blood staining the white carpet below. The wind picked up again knowing the battle was getting more and more dangerous.

Huckle sprinkled two speckles of Dantra dust on the ear, followed by two drops of swirling blue liquid from a bottle in his cloak. The ear turned on the floor and started spinning like a fairground ride. The Tipplings looked on as the ear started a mini tornado. Something inside the tornado started growing. Strontar had never seen such evil magic before and stepped back. Snow particles flew in every direction as the tornado grew bigger. The Grotchins stepped back as the Master held out his arms and started chanting his dark evil magic.

Grotchins curse I give to you,
A beast that comes from liquid blue.
Animal from Gan, with hate,
Destroy the Tipplings, that's their fate.

The swirling tornado spun faster and faster. The snowflakes lifted off the ground and ripped into the Tipplings' faces like needles. The Master laughed horribly as he knew this would destroy his enemy one by one in unimaginable horror. The swirling stopped abruptly leaving a large tube of what looked like smoke directly in front of the Tippling army. Strontar rubbed his eyes removing all the snow needles that had embedded in his pupils. All the Tippling men looked on, waiting for what was going to happen next. Huckle smirked again as the wind picked up and snow fell onto the battleground.

"Kill them all" he ordered as the beast in front of him stepped from the smoke tube.

As the Tipplings looked on in shock, an eight-foot-tall creature with dark greasy skin glared back at them with massive razor-sharp teeth. The creature with his mighty muscular body stood and gazed at its food source. Huckle grinned to himself and smiled at his creation, the Beast of Gan. The beast lived on blood and warm Tippling blood would fill his stomach nicely.

The Tipplings all stepped back in horror. Strontar held up his wand and threw a spell hitting creature directly in its face. The Tippling looked on anxiously. The creature just glared and didn't move a muscle. His sharp teeth gnashed together like two mechanical digger buckets and sounded just as loud. It stood still and awaited its orders.

The snow started falling again as Strontar stepped back, his magic useless against this giant of a beast. The wind picked up as Huckle's black hair seemed to leave his cloaked hood and dance with the pure white snow. The lights in the mud huts flickered on and off, was this the last time these lights would be lit? Huckle stepped forward and tapped his creation on its shoulder.

"Kill them, kill them all, every single one of them"

The creature gnashed its teeth again and suddenly ran towards the enemy in front of him. Strontar tried a spell again but the creature just shrugged it off. Was this it? Was this the end of the Tipplings?

Strontar turned to his companions and told them to stand firm and fight for their lives and for their families' lives. The beast roared towards them, snow flying up from the ground beneath its long sharp toes.

Suddenly, from nowhere, Zezma, Daniel, Tim and Taff appeared. Zezma threw his first spell and hit the beast directly in its chest. The beast stopped as if it had hit a brick wall. Huckle looked on in amazement and then grimaced. Alfren stepped forward and started to run towards Zezma, but once again Zezma stopped him in tracks, creating an invisible barrier between the Tipplings and the Master.

Zezma cast another spell from his wand, sending Huckle flying to the snowy ground with an almighty crash. Huckle had never been put on his back before and for once felt weakness in his magic. Zezma ordered Strontar and his soldiers to move forward and show strength.

"Todays the day evil leaves our land" shouted the Tippling, moving forward with Daniel, Tim and Taff close to his side.

Huckle rose to his feet and shook himself. This was a fight he wasn't prepared for but was more than willing to take. He lifted his wand and threw a spell, hitting the invisible barrier with an almighty flash. The spell bounced off the barrier hitting a Tippling house in the corner of the street which exploded into dust.

He threw another and then another, still he couldn't get through the barrier. The creature from Gan and all the Grotchins tried to break the barrier but it seemed impossible. Zezma's magic was stronger than Huckle had ever imagined.

The two moons appeared from behind the dark clouds and watched the spectacle from the heavens above. Flashes of light exploded into the night's sky as the battle continued. Huckle couldn't believe this Tippling's power and his mind moved into overdrive thinking of the Tippling's weakness.

Then suddenly he shouted at the top of his voice "Helta".

The snow stopped in the sky as did everything in Fentwell for a split second. Zezma looked on nervously, holding his wand in his right hand. He knew Helta was in the Master's grip.

"Give me Strontar, Zezma, and I will give you your sister back" ordered Huckle.

Zezma looked to his elder who stood at his side next to Daniel. The elder stepped forward and spoke as the snow started falling again.

"Take me and release your sister" he said.

Zezma stood tall knowing that if Strontar was taken he would be the next in line to take the Tipplings to safety. The Master looked at his Grotchins and grinned. Alfren grinned back knowing the Master's tricks.

Zezma knew he had to take Huckle's offer or he might never get Helta back again. He held up his wand and cast his barrier releasing spell. A hole suddenly appeared like a tunnel for Strontar to walk through and face his doom. But Huckle was truly evil and had other ideas.

Suddenly the beast charged through the tunnel smashing Strontar to the ground, racing forward to take Zezma. Zezma quickly closed the tunnel and smashed a fireball against the creature sending it flying backwards, but still the beast came. It rose to its feet and charged forward again.

Zezma sent another flashing light, hurling the creature against one of the small houses with one almighty smash. Huckle and his Grotchins watched through the barrier as Zezma and the beast battled against each other. Daniel, Tim and Taff could only look on as the battle erupted. Zezma quickly reached in his cloth bag and brought out a sharp star-shaped stone.

This was the millionth stone that had been counted by Zezma. The millionth stone to be found by any Tippling had many powers, but this was totally unknown to Huckle. Zezma raised his hand and as the beast got close enough, he threw it as hard as he could, hitting the beast directly in its stomach. The creature suddenly stopped, clutching its stomach in agony and looked around for his Master's help. Huckle looked on with his mouth wide open, this magic was impossible he thought to himself as the beast roared in agony.

Zezma raised his wand and a flash of light hit the beast directly where the stone had hit. The Tippling spoke, commanding the stone to do its worst. The beast battled with all his might as the spell worked its magic. Huckle froze and watched in awe.

Magic stone of Fentwell land,
Fireflies of a million send,
Inject your young and taste its blood,
Evil shall be gone for good.

With that the firefly spell of a million flies ripped

into the beast's blood vessels like a virus, injecting its blood with devastating effect. The beast rolled over in agony as the flies sucked the blood from its veins. Within two minutes the great beast of Gan lay dead on the blood red snowy ground. All the Tipplings cheered as Strontar smiled and raised his wand into the air. Huckle looked on with fear in his eyes, no one had ever before created magic like this against him. He ordered his soldiers to quickly retreat as the cold wind blew into his dark black eyes. Huckle knew he had a fight on his hands and would have to get back to his lair as soon as possible for some more potions. This Tippling's magic was going to be hard to defeat.

Huckle jumped up onto one of his black stallions and raced off towards the Brittle Mountains of Smor with his soldiers following closely behind. The pathway was covered in a trail of snowy dust as evil left the city. The Tipplings all cheered loudly again, as did Tim and Daniel, as they watched the Master and his Grotchins leave the small city.

Zezma asked Strontar to fetch him three horses which he did immediately. Zezma knew he had to complete his task, or the Master would be back. Zezma, Daniel, Tim and Taff jumped onto the horses and quickly followed the evil out of the city to finish off this battle once and for all.

Chapter 14
The Frozen Lake

Zezma raced along the pathway as fast as his horse could carry him. The snowy dust from Huckle and the Grotchins in front of them got closer and closer with every stride. The Tippling's horses raced the fastest race they had ever entered as the two moons of Fentwell were now wide awake and ready to watch the main event of the night's fighting.

The snow had stopped, and the night sky was now clear of clouds as ten million starry spectators looked on anxiously. Tonight, there would be only one winner. The pathway up the mountain was now thick with snow and the Tippling and his friends dismounted from their horses, as had Huckle and his Grotchins earlier.

"Huckle" shouted the Tippling as his voice echoed into the valley and mountains above.

Huckle looked around, seeing his enemy moving closer and closer as the spectators in the sky watched on. Huckle ordered all his Grotchins except Alfren to wait behind the next corner and destroy the Tippling at whatever cost.

"Do not let him or the Earth boy pass" commanded Huckle "or I will destroy you. My orders are" Kill Kill Kill."

Huckle and Alfren scurried off and moved closer towards the lair. The Master shook with fear as Alfren helped him up the pathway. Only thirty yards to go and he and his loyal servant would be safe.

Zezma knew if Huckle got back to his lair and closed the crack in the mountainside, there would be no way in. Huckle could then use his magic and return to Dantra where he could replenish his powers and return with an army of creatures.

Zezma moved on up the mountain pathway with his friends, passing the almighty great black stallions as they stood on the pathway. Steam rose from their armoured backs and entered the night's sky like a smoke machine. The Grotchins hid around the corner waiting for their battle with the Tippling. The largest and most horrible looking Grotchin ever seen stood in front with his large silver sword in his hand. His long sharp teeth glistened in the starry night as Whizzer and Donzo stood close behind him with the remaining Grotchins.

Ice hung onto the large jagged sword as the moonlight twinkled along its sharp edge, waiting to slice anything in half that approached it. The corner came closer as Zezma wiped the sweat from his brow and moved forward on the slippery pathway. The Grotchins were ready with their swords and ready to please their Master.

Zezma and Daniel turned around the corner first, as the Grotchin snarled and clenched his teeth together. The two moons again looked down and shone brightly ready for the fighting to begin. The monster Grotchin hissed like a king cobra snake then took a step forward towards Zezma and Daniel. The Grotchin stench entered Daniel's nostrils again and he gagged, looking on at the beast that stood in front of him. Zezma stopped and knew this battle had to be quick as Huckle was moving closer up the steep pathway nearer to his safety.

The wand in his right hand cast the first spell as the horrible Grotchin ran at full speed in their direction with his sword held high ready for battle. The first flashing spell hit him directly in his neck and the creature fell to the ground with a crash. The snow covered his face as the second spell sent him flying over the cliff's edge into the frozen lake below. Huckle heard the Grotchin yells and pulled his black cloak over his head as he raced towards his lair.

Zezma raced over to the edge of the cliff and watched as the Grotchin fell to his horrible icy cold death below. The Grotchin's screams soon faded as he landed on one of the large stone skewers. Whizzer and Donzo gazed on then sprinted forward towards Daniel, Tim and Taff, followed by their small army of Grotchins. Daniel and his friends stood helpless as the Grotchins smashed their swords against the icy pathway with anger.

Zezma quickly returned to his position but his magic seemed to fade a little. He cast another spell. This time Whizzer and Donzo dodged the spell but it hit the other three Grotchins, sending them over the edge of the cliff like their elder into their dark death hole. The Master heard more screams, but this time took no notice, he knew his life of a thousand years was at threat and edged on.

The Grotchins were now only yards away from their enemies and Zezma's magic was fading fast. He cast a double spell, but it was weak. It hit both Whizzer and Donzo directly in their heads. The Grotchins stopped immediately with a jolt. Stiffened by Zezma's magic, they couldn't move a muscle. Suddenly they started rising upwards towards the two moons above them. Then like ghosts floating, the Tippling directed them with his wand towards the cliff's edge. The two Grotchins were now about thirty foot in the air screaming as they battled with the spell. Luckily it held strong.

Zezma collapsed to the floor letting go of the spell and the Grotchin brothers dropped over the edge of the cliff screaming like banshees. One hit the sharp stone skewers below with a scream that entered Alfren's ears with dread. The other fell crashing onto the lake's rocks below. Alfren let go of his Master's arm and stopped, he let out a scream, a horrible death scream which chilled anybody or anything that heard it. His brothers were dead, and he wanted revenge. Huckle grabbed his solider by his snow-covered cloth cloak and dragged him further up the snowy steep pathway with him.

Daniel and Tim helped Zezma up from the cold floor. He seemed absolutely exhausted and Daniel was worried.

"We must defeat him today" said the Tippling putting herbs and blue liquid from his bag into his frozen lipped mouth. Zezma gained a little strength and the gang moved on.

Huckle screamed from the mountainside above as he was stopped in his tracks by the avalanche earlier which had blocked the pathway. He sent an almighty flash of light from his wand lighting up the whole valley below. The Tipplings below in Smor watched as the light show above shone in their faces like bonfire night. All the Tipplings knew this was a battle that would either save or conquer Fentwell forever.

Huckle sent another almighty flash of light but the pathway wouldn't clear and the Master and his solider were stuck. Alfren grinned knowing this was a chance to revenge his brother's killers and gnashed his razor-sharp teeth together. Huckle collected items from his cloak and placed them carefully hidden on to the pathway then told his solider to dig a hole in the snow and hide. They hid together in the snowdrift as the Tippling and his Earth friends moved closer up the pathway towards their enemy. Zezma ate more herbs and gained some more strength, but nothing like he had had earlier.

Zezma's strength continued to improve as he walked up the mountainside. The wind picked up a little leaving the stench of the Grotchins in their death beds below filling the Earth boy's nostrils once again. The pathway grew narrower as Huckle and Alfren hid quietly in their snow covered cocoon. The two moons of Fentwell shone the brightest ever waiting patiently for the result of the main event, just like all the Tipplings in the city below. Zezma looked down from the edge of the cliff at his beautiful city and knew he had to succeed tonight, or everyone would be slaughtered and the Tipplings would be gone forever. The glow of the torches glistened orange in the tiny snowy city. All was quiet as if in the centre of a Hurricane, but the Hurricane was soon about to rip the land of Fentwell apart.

Chapter 15
Thirteen Words

Huckle and Alfren hid in the snowdrift hole as the Tippling and his friends edged closer and closer. Alfren, like a dog on a leash, waited patiently, ready to slaughter his enemy. Daniel walked in front as the first of Huckle's magic hit him. His legs buckled as long black leech like creatures raced up his legs biting him everywhere. His legs bled heavily as Zezma threw a spell of salt from his wand killing the leeches instantly. The battle had begun.

Zezma helped Daniel to his feet as the dead leeches hissed on the ground in the salt spell. Blood dripped from his legs, but the battle was getting nearer. The next Huckle spell sent shivers into Zezma's core. In front of him stood Helta begging him to give himself up to the Master.

Was this the decider? Was Huckle's spell strong enough?

Helta told Zezma if he gave himself up, she would be saved. The Tippling was weak and Huckle knew it. He decided to take his chance. Zezma was transfixed and ready to commit his life to the Master. Huckle and Alfren looked on through a small hole in their hideaway as Zezma fell to his knees. Huckle grinned and burst out of his hideout with both hands up in the air.

"JOIN ME TIPPLING" screamed the evil Master, as the valley below and the two moons shook with fear.

"JOIN ME AND WE CAN CONQUER THE WORLD".

Alfren stepped out of the snowdrift and waited for his command to kill the Earth boys and their mutt of a dog. His gnashing teeth ground together like a rabid wolf. Zezma was finished, he had no strength left, was this it? He knees buckled and he fell to the ground and held his hands to his head. Huckle knew he had won and walked over to the gang knowing the battle was over. He glared down at his enemy who knelt in front of him. Evil froze Fentwell for a minute. The Tippling families below felt it and gazed up, awaiting their fate. Huckle took off his black cloak and shook it in the Tippling's face, he then looked at the Earth boy.

He snarled then suddenly with his left arm knocked Daniel to the ground. Daniel bled heavily from his nose as Tim and Taff looked on. With his staff held firmly in his right hand, he raised it to the two moons above his head and bellowed at the city below,

"FENTWELL IS MINE, ALL MINE."

The Tipplings below all looked at each other with horror in their eyes. Zezma's parents cried as all the Tipplings quickly fled, petrified, to their hideouts. The two moons also suddenly hid behind the clouds as the

Master finally took control. The Fentwell sky started crying snow again as the cold eerie wind blew in the Master's long hair. The beautiful land of Fentwell would be desolate in less than an hour and Huckle's creatures would devour everything in sight.

Alfren waited and waited frothing at the mouth for his two brother's revenge. His revenge was going to be slow and violent as Huckle spoke to him.

"Wait my loyal servant and cherish every second. Zezma is mine but do what you want with the others".

Daniel and Tim sat together with Taff at their side. This was the end. Huckle leaned over and told Zezma to rise and await his doom.

The Tippling looked again at his city below and then rose looking deep into his enemy's eyes. Huckle laughed then hit him to the ground with his wand. Zezma rose, with Daniel by his side. Huckle laughed calling Daniel pathetic and looked straight into the Earth boy's eyes.

Daniel remembered Zezma telling him never to look into the Master's eyes but something inside him told him to do so. He glared deep into the dark two holes that seemed to go deeper and deeper into the depths of the Master's soul. Huckle gazed back but the Master's smile soon turned to shock as Daniel kept gazing back with his bright blue eyes.

Never had anyone gazed back at Huckle like this before. Huckle's legs suddenly buckled and he fell to his knees. Daniel found strength and walked forward and continued gazing into the Master's eyes. Alfren looked on waiting for his chance, one command and the Earth boy would be ripped to shreds as if he was in a shredding machine.

Daniel leaned over towards the Master then whispered thirteen words into his right ear. Huckle froze hearing the words and looked at the Earth boy with total fear. Alfren snapped at Daniel but somehow Zezma froze him to the spot with the last but one spell left in his body. Huckle looked confused as snow particles fell onto to his hooded cloak. The battle was easily won but what was happening. Alfren was frozen to the spot, his eyes moving widely in his head but unable to move. Zezma looked on in amazement at the Earth boy. Then with his last bit of strength started to cast his last spell for the future of Fentwell.

Net of snow all strong and white,
Cover my enemies with all your might.
Don't let go until I say.
One last spell I hope, I pray.

The snow listened then fell quicker and quicker from the Fentwell sky creating a large oval-shaped white net above Huckle's and Alfren's heads. The Master and the Grotchin could do nothing, the net hovered above the enemy as the Tippling held his wand up high, then brought it down with a crash. The Master and the Grotchin were now going nowhere, the snow net was as strong as steel and covered them completely. Zezma raised the net and his enemies into the air and edged it towards the cliff's edge.

The Master screamed the loudest scream ever

heard in Fentwell and suddenly knew his fate was in the hands of the Tippling. Zezma walked over with Daniel as the net hovered above the cliff's edge for what seemed like an eternity. One swoop down of the wand and it was over. Or was it?

Huckle begged, but begging was no good now. Zezma spun his wand around his head and commanded the snowy ice net to open. The net slowly started releasing its catch of the day. First fell the great Grotchin Alfren, screaming as his voice faded into the depths below, followed closely by Huckle himself. The frozen lake below was ready to devour the evil pair. The skies brightened as the two moons shone down just as the two smashed together against the frozen lake below. They both lay dead on the icy lake as thick red blood poured from Huckle's head and stained the ice. Alfren's eyes were stuck wide open, black and cold with his death. Huckle's cold eyes gazed up into the heavens above but then suddenly blinked. Huckle was not dead!

In agony he lifted himself to his knees and looked up towards the cliff's edge above him. The Tippling and the Earth boy couldn't believe it. Huckle's battered body now covered in blood stood up. He held up his staff in his hand just as the ice below him creaked and cracked. The Master wasn't dead but in one minute he would be. He moved one foot and suddenly the lake of Derelin took him. The ice beneath him shattered like a large pane of glass and he and his great Grotchin sank into the depths of the bottomless black lake. Daniel fell to his knees in disbelief and Zezma helped him back up to his feet.

The Master and his Grotchin were dead.

The land of Fentwell lit up as the two sunk deeper and deeper into the dark bottomless lake. The two moons soon disappeared to early morning daylight. The sun shone through the clouds as the Tipplings in Smor came out of hiding and looked up to the Brittle Mountains above. Zezma gazed at the lake below as the crack in the ice quickly reformed letting no one or nothing out. He looked at his friends and couldn't believe they had defeated the evil Master. He grasped Daniel by his arm as he and his friends headed back to the city, battered and bruised but still alive.

All the Tippling children had regained their memories as the evil Huckle's spell broke with his icy death. Happiness was back in the city. Zezma and his gang returned down the mountain to the small city as Zezma's mother and sister threw their arms around him. Tipplings cheered as Zezma and his friends walked through the streets of Smor like heroes. The snow slowly disappeared from the city as the sun warmed up the land. Zezma sat in his house with his Earth friends and thanked them for saving his land. Daniel, Tim and Taff were given a drink of Fentwell water by Zezma's mother and instantly seemed better. Tim looked at Daniel and asked if they could please go home now as Zezma laughed and told his friends he would return them immediately. Daniel stood to his feet and grinned at his new Tippling friend; he knew he had to go home.

They walked to the doorway and turned to say goodbye. All the Tipplings cheered as Daniel glared up at the Brittle Mountains of Smor. Snow and ice still lay thick on the mountains as it had done for centuries. The lake Derelin would always be in his mind as would this story. They walked a little further as Zezma's father gave them all a small black stone from the stream of Asbadan.

"This will help you on your journey," said the Tippling with a kind and caring voice.

Zezma and his father walked the heroes towards a large oak tree by a stream and told them to sit down as close to the tree as possible.

"This magic would only take two seconds and then you will back on Earth". explained Zenton.

Daniel sat by the great tree with Tim and Taff and looked on at the beautiful land thinking he would never set foot there again.

Zezma looked on as his friends were about to go home. He leaned over and asked Daniel quietly in his ear what he had said to disturb Huckle in such a way. Daniel shook his head and said, "I'll tell you next time". Then grinned.

Zezma smiled as his father poured Asbadan water on his friends' heads and started chanting the last of this Tippling's magic tale.

Oh great water of Fentwell stream.
Take them back from this nightmare dream.
A dream that's true and will never pass,
A journey safe this spell I cast.

Within a second there was a bright flash and they were back. Rain poured onto Daniel's face like a waterfall. The boys were indeed back, no longer sat next to the oak in Fentwell but sat next to the great fallen oak in Bont. The boys looked on as Taff ran in the direction of his home.

Three days had passed in Fentwell but only five minutes of Earth time. The boys stood up gazing at their cold surroundings. The storm was still as strong as ever and the lights still flickered in the houses and also the Highwayman's Arms. An old lady walked past with a hooded coat on and looked at them sternly. For one minute they thought it was a Grotchin or Huckle himself, but that was impossible, they were dead.

Daniel looked at his watch and saw they had one minute to get back to school. They ran down the street soaked to the bone and reached the school gates. They gazed at each other not knowing what to say when a familiar voice suddenly shouted from the staff room.

"Hawthorn, Thomas, will you get in NOW"

This brought a grin to their faces knowing they were safely home. The boys grinned at each other then parted and headed back towards their classrooms. Daniel with his skinny body shivering moved down the corridors soaked to the bone. Rain dripped off his jacket and fell onto the old wooden flooring. The school's heating was off again leaving the school corridors freezing cold.

In front of him walking down the cold dark corridor leading to his art lesson was Smithson, wearing a long dark cloak. His heart missed a beat thinking of Huckle. He stopped as the figure turned around. It wasn't Smithson at all or any of the teachers in the whole school. It was Huckle himself, sending the boy a message from beyond his icy cold grave.

Huckle wasn't dead at all, just frozen solid in the deep cold icy lake of Derelin. Only Huckle's black eyes could move in the deep black cold water. The vision spoke.

"Beware of me Earth boy and beware of your dreams".

The figure grimaced and quickly faded into smoke in the cold school corridor. The voice spoke again as the smoke swirled around and headed towards an open window.

"I will be back for you Hawthorn, and the Tippling.

Soon very very Soon!"

Printed in Great Britain
by Amazon

69948076R00108